Ebola K

Book One

of the Ebola K Trilogy

By

Bobby Adair

http://www.bobbyadair.com

http://www.facebook.com/BobbyAdairAuthor

The eBook version of Ebola K is available free on Kindle, iTunes, Barnes & Noble, and Smashwords.

The audiobook version of Ebola K
will appear on Audible in Fall 2014

Cover Design and Layout

Alex Saskalidis, a.k.a. 187designz

Editing, Proofreading

Kat Kramer
Cathy Moeschet
Linda Tooch

Technical Consultant

John Cummings

eBook and Print Formatting

Kat Kramer

Preface

My son spent the summer of 2013 in Uganda and was the inspiration for one of the book's characters, Austin Cooper. I was so moved by some of the stories he came back with that I started to write them out as a record of the events. But as things turn out in my mind, the true stories got sucked into a series of what-if questions along with the concern I've had with Ebola since I first heard of it after the 1976 outbreaks in Zaire. And of course that was rolled into another of my favorite subjects, post-apocalyptic fiction.

Hence, this story—as anyone reading in 2014 knows—occurs contemporaneously with the largest Ebola outbreak in African history. I adjusted some of the details of the story in order to pin it to recent news events.

Except for the Ebola virus mutating into an airborne strain as it does in the story (which is purely fictional), all of the information presented about Ebola and its effects is accurate according to published medical documents and historical news records. On that note, I am occasionally contacted by readers who have expertise in different areas, and if you have information that contributes to the accuracy of this story, I encourage you to contact me through my website.

Keeping in mind the reality of the world we live in, Ebola is a terrible disease that—even as I write this story—is gruesomely killing people just like you and me, except for the fact that they weren't lucky enough to be born in an affluent country. I read an article last night about a shortage of medical supplies available to nurses, doctors, and volunteers treating patients in Liberia. Because even the most basic protective gear—such as gloves—isn't available, people are putting their lives at risk in order to help others.

While I harbor no illusions about fixing that problem or curing the world's ills through a donation, I'd encourage anyone interested in helping to consider providing a measure of assistance to people unfortunate enough to be afflicted with this and other diseases. Hence, a portion of the proceeds from these books will be donated to that cause. If any of you feel moved to assist, I'll post a set of links on my website that will direct you to charitable organizations that engage in these sorts of activities. Every little bit helps.

<u>http://www.bobbyadair.com/Ebola</u>

Getting back to business, this first book in the trilogy is provided at no charge, with two more modestly priced books to follow. This is a strategy I use to give readers a chance to try out the first book in a series risk-free. Without the burden of a large publisher and shareholders to please, indie authors have the flexibility to market their work in creative ways. As we experience a paradigm shift from traditional publishing, you might notice a large number of high-quality works at lower prices or even free. You'll find many new authors who are excited to get their work in your hands, so don't let the price—or lack of one—affect your perception of the quality of their work.

With that said, your feedback and reviews are valued and appreciated, so if you enjoy the book, please take a moment and write a short review and leave it on the website where you obtained the book. Links are provided at the end. Also don't forget to "Like" my Facebook page... we have a lot of fun and really enjoy interacting with readers.

And just as the readers in my Slow Burn series have

enjoyed the suspense left at the end of each book—spoiler alert—there *is* a cliffhanger at the end of Ebola K: Book 1.

Enjoy,
Bobby

Chapter 1

"Seems like ever since you got to Uganda, you can't stop talking. But today, you're quiet. What's up?"

Austin Cooper made a noncommittal sound into his cell phone and thought about whether to tell his dad the thoughts that were bothering him.

"Did you go bungee jumping into the Nile again?"

Nothing like that.

"Camping with the coffee farmers up on Mt. Elgon?"

"No." Austin took a long, slow breath. It was going to be hard.

With his elbows on the rough-hewn piece of wood lashed between two poles that passed for a table in the little shop, Austin looked out at people who were passing on the street. He spotted Rashid talking to a boda driver. He ran a finger around the remains of the ugali and cabbage on his plate. "I've been in Mbale all week. When I first got here, I was walking down the street. It was pretty crowded and all. I was going down to a market to get some fruit and I saw this kid on a rooftop up ahead."

Into the pause, Austin's dad, Paul Cooper, said, "Yeah?"

There was no good way to ease into it, so Austin simply said it. "Somebody pushed him off."

The phone was silent over the space of a few breaths. "Someone pushed the kid off the roof? Did he get hurt?"

"Yeah, pretty badly. But nobody stopped to help. All the people ignored him and walked by."

"What?" Paul was surprised.

"That's how it is here," said Austin. "He was a street kid. They're like some kind of a lower caste. They're orphans.

1

They live on the edge of town in the dumps and eat scraps. Most of them have AIDS. "

"And those are the ones you teach?"

"Yes."

"Was he one of your students?" Paul asked.

"No. I teach in Kapchorwa." Austin looked out to the street again. Rashid was negotiating with a boda driver for a ride back to Kapchorwa. Rashid always did the negotiating with Austin out of sight. They'd learned early in their stay that Austin's blue eyes and blond hair always got them the mzungu price. Rashid, being Arabic, got a better deal.

"I can't keep the names of those places straight. What happened to the kid?"

Austin choked up. Just thinking about the story brought unexpected emotion. He faked a cough to cover it. "I couldn't...I had to do something."

"What happened?" Paul asked.

"I picked him up and carried him to the hospital."

Paul was at a loss for words. After several long moments, he said, "I'm proud of you."

"The hospital wouldn't take him because he was a street kid."

"You're shitting me," Paul's voice was full of disgust.

Austin was unfazed by the profanity. His dad never had much respect for the concept of good and bad words. "No. The only way they'd take him is if I paid. It took pretty much the rest of my money. I'm nearly broke." Austin hadn't intended to add that last line. The opportunity to teach for the summer in Uganda had cost them both a bit more than they could afford.

Without hesitation, Paul said, "I'll transfer some money

into your account, okay? I'm proud of you. I really am. You're turning into a pretty good person. I think this summer in Uganda is good for you."

"Thanks." Austin wondered about whether to tell his dad the next part. But Paul wasn't a worrier, not like Austin's mom. "There's more."

"Yeah?"

"I stayed at the hospital with him for four days. I didn't think they'd let him stay if I left. But after the fourth day, I kinda got comfortable with the staff and felt I could trust them."

"Uh-huh."

"So I left the hospital for a while and went out to get something to eat." At that point, Austin had to fake another cough. It was the first time he'd told the story and the emotions—just days old—were still raw.

With growing concern, Paul asked, "What happened?"

"They kicked him out of the hospital." Another slow, deep breath. "I went out looking for him. It was a gang that pushed him off the roof."

"Like Bloods and Crips?" Paul asked.

"No," said Austin. "The country has a lot of misguided groups who are doing some really crappy things in the name of religion. The Lord's Resistance Movement is the one you hear about putting kids into sex slavery or forcing them into their army. They think these street kids are sinners or unclean or something. Dad, they caught him and castrated him. They left him in the street."

"Jesus."

"He bled to death."

It was Paul's turn to fake a cough to cover *his* emotions. "Are you okay?"

"Not at first. I'm okay now, I think."

"I'm really proud of you for helping the kid," Paul said again.

"Thanks."

"Do you think you're in any danger?" Paul asked.

"How's that?" Austin was wondering if he'd been wrong about his dad being a worrier. Perhaps his stepmom had converted him. Not good.

Paul said, "Maybe from the gang that killed the kid. Do you think they'll come after you for taking him to the hospital?"

"No, they pretty much leave mzungus alone."

"Mzungus?"

"Sorry. It's their word for white people. They kind of have special rules for us. I'll be fine."

"Okay. Don't tell your mother about this until you get back. You know she wasn't jazzed about you going to Uganda in the first place, and now that she knows about this Ebola thing in Sierra Leone, she's kind of freaked out."

"Uh-huh."

"Don't trivialize it," Paul said. "You know how much she worries. She'd go nuts with you there for another month, thinking you could get hurt."

"I won't say anything."

"When was the last time you talked to her?"

"A couple of weeks ago."

"Call your mom when you get off the phone with me, okay?"

Austin glanced out toward the street. Rashid was shuffling and looking around, making a show of his restlessness. The impatience of the Ugandan man beside him looked real. "I can't. I think my boda guy won't wait."

"A boda, that's the motorcycle thing, right?"

"It is a motorcycle, a motorcycle taxi. You know, they have those long seats like you used to have in the seventies so they can squeeze more than two people on them."

Paul ignored the dig about his age. "You did get that email from your stepmom, right?"

"Heidi sent me a bunch. Which one?"

"Probably one you didn't read."

Austin chuckled. "I didn't read most of them."

Paul laughed. "Look, I know how she can be a pain, but she did find a lot of good information about Uganda. You really should read them."

"CliffsNotes?"

"I'm not going to summarize her emails."

Austin laughed. "Why not? She's *your* wife."

His dad laughed, too. "Just be careful on the bodas. The State Department or wherever she got the information said to stay off the bodas because people always get hurt on them."

"Everybody here has a boda scar." Austin laughed again.

"I feel *so* much better."

"Don't tell Mom about the boda then."

"I'm not saying anything to your mother. The less she knows, the happier she'll be. Is the boda guy taking you back to Kapchorwa?"

"Yes."

"How far is it?"

"I don't know. An hour and a half?"

"Super." Paul said it with plenty of sarcasm.

"Anyway, we need to get going. This is the first boda

driver we found that'll make the trip. The others don't think they'll get back here before dark."

"I feel *so* much better knowing the accident-prone motorcycle taxi driver will be in a hurry." More sarcasm.

Austin laughed—the laugh of someone who was twenty years old and still believed that bad things only happened to other people.

"Keep in touch okay? At least email me every week so I know what's going on."

"Is Heidi bothering you about not hearing from me often enough?" Austin smiled.

"I do tend to pick 'em."

Austin said, "I don't have the Internet or phone service in the village."

"I know, you've told me. But you come into town every week, right?" Paul asked.

"Maybe not next week. We're supposed to go camping in the mountains again."

"Let me know when you get back, okay?"

"Yeah. I gotta go."

Chapter 2

Austin walked out of the shade of the little restaurant's thatched roof and waived a thanks to the proprietor.

Rashid pointed to a spot in the center of the boda's long motorcycle seat. "You're riding in the middle."

"No, I'm not," Austin answered. "I'm paying."

"This is your friend?" The boda driver asked.

Rashid told him, "He's got the money. You want it or not?" To Austin he said, "I negotiated. You should sit in the middle."

"You can get your own if you want," said Austin. "Your dad's got, like, a bazillion dollars, right? It's not my fault you're always broke."

Rashid's brow furrowed. He shook his head and raised a finger to his lips. He leaned in close so that only Austin could hear what he was about to say. "I told you, keep that quiet. You could get me kidnapped."

"Sorry," Austin whispered back. In his normal tone, he said, "Get on, let's get going."

The boda driver said, "It's a long way to Kapchorwa. Money first."

Austin paid him.

"Something you should know before we go," Rashid said.

"Yeah?" Austin asked.

"The road is blocked."

"It is," the boda driver said. "My cousin told me."

Rashid continued, "The military closed down that road and a bunch of others in the eastern districts."

Austin wondered if the driver was steering the

conversation toward a renegotiation of the price. "Why?"

"Ebola," answered the driver.

"Here?" Austin didn't want to believe it.

Rashid shook his head and shot the driver a look that told him to be quiet. "Rumors. The Ebola outbreak is in Sierra Leone. Just rumors."

"So, what are we doing, then?" Austin asked.

The boda driver pointed north. "I know a way on a trail."

"How close can we get?"

"You'll see the village from where I drop you," the boda driver answered.

Austin said, "I can see Kapchorwa from the top of Mt. Elgon and that's, like, ten miles away."

"A kilometer, maybe less," said the driver.

"Okay. Let's go." Austin walked toward the bike.

The driver threw a leg over his motorcycle.

To Rashid, Austin motioned, "You're next."

"I hate being in the middle," Rashid complained.

"Trust me. It's just as uncomfortable for me, but it's what we can afford."

Chapter 3

Forty minutes on the dusty, bumpy, red clay road was bad, but the single-track through the bush was worse.

The boda driver turned to yell over the whine of the engine, "Hold on."

They bounced over a hump in the trail and Austin nearly went off the back.

Rashid looked over his shoulder at Austin. "Not so tight."

"I don't want to fall," Austin told him.

Rashid sneezed.

"Damn, dude." Austin wiped his face on Rashid's shirt. "You got that all over me."

"You should have let me ride in back."

"What? You sneezed on me on purpose?"

Rashid sneezed again.

"Damn. Turn your head, Rashid."

"I did!"

"Turn it the other way. I'm on your left."

"Why didn't you say so?"

The jungle on both sides of the trail closed in. Leaves big and small brushed Austin's knees. Thin branches scraped. And it all grew thicker the higher up the side of the mountain the trail wound. The boda's engine whined as it pulled the three young men up a particularly steep section of the trail, and the tires skidded down muddy tracks as the driver uselessly squeezed the brakes until the wheels locked. Miraculously, he kept the motorcycle upright.

More than once Austin wanted to pull his phone out of his pocket to check the time and see how much longer they had to risk breaking their bones on the trail, but feared that pulling one hand away from Rashid's waist would result in him being bounced off the back of the bike.

They'd been on the trail for at least a half hour, maybe twice that long, when it smoothed out on a gentle upward slope. They were going slow enough by then that Austin figured he could have a conversation with Rashid and not have the words lost in the wind. "Hey, what do you think of this Ebola thing?"

"You sound scared," said Rashid, looking back over his shoulder with a grin.

"Worried is a better word."

Rashid laughed. "A billion people in Africa, and maybe a few thousand cases of Ebola ever, and you think you're in trouble."

Put that way, it made Austin's fear of Ebola embarrassing. Nevertheless, he said, "Ebola kills everybody who gets it."

Rashid laughed again. "Not *everybody*."

The boda rode up on a crest and the jungle thinned. They were well up on the north slope of Mt. Elgon. Below, Kapchorwa's houses and huts seemed to grow out of the intersection of a few dirt roads—some short, some snaking off east or west. Paving for the roads hadn't made it from the capital out to the distant districts yet. And the Kapchorwa District, bordered on the east by Kenya with its hundred thousand farmers, was just about as far from Kampala as one could get and still be in Uganda.

The boda driver stopped and announced, "Here."

Austin stepped off the bike. "Thanks."

Rashid got off, hitched up his pants, and adjusted his man parts. "Next time, I'll get my own boda."

"You do that, Rashid." Austin reached into his pocket to pull out a few more shillings as a tip, but the boda driver was already hurrying to get back up the trail and apparently away from Kapchorwa. He flashed a white palm in a wave and smiled as he revved the whiny engine to speed back up the bumpy trail.

Still thinking about the Ebola virus, Austin said, "He got out of here in a hurry."

Rashid watched the boda driver zip back up the trail, not seeming to care how quickly the boda left. "It'll be dark soon."

Austin looked west toward the sun sinking over the brown and green plain. The smoke of a few fires drifted up and dissolved in the wind. They were too large to be cooking fires, but too small to be wild fires. Probably charcoal production. At least, that was the guess that Austin attached to forested spots in the distance that leaked smoldering gray into the sky. He stopped staring at the vista and started walking down the trail. Rashid went along.

The small town of Kapchorwa, with its hundred or so dwellings, sheds, and businesses, seemed quiet. Looking down the slope, Austin didn't see anyone moving around, nor did he hear the distant shrill sounds of children playing before dinner. He did smell peanuts roasting—groundnuts, to the locals—along with the savory smell of onions cooking. He realized he was hungry again.

Down on the village's main road, an overturned semi-tractor-trailer still lay as it had since rolling over during Austin's first week of teaching. Every day since, when it wasn't raining, village kids played on the overturned vehicle. And though no rain clouds were in the sky, the kids were absent.

Halfway down the slope, they left the meandering trail and cut across a lush sweet potato field.

They neared a house, mud-walled on a wooden frame under a tin roof rusted as red as wet clay. It stood alone among the crops. A rope draped with wrinkled clothes was strung from one corner of the house to a lone tree. Plastic tubs of different colors—all-purpose and dirty—leaned against the walls outside. From the deep shadows inside the open doorway of the hovel, a pair of silently wary eyes watched Austin and Rashid pass.

Softly, Rashid said, "That man is frightened."

Austin looked back at Rashid. "Of us?"

Rashid shook his head.

"How do you know?" Austin asked.

"Are you joking? You couldn't see the fright in his eyes?"

"I think you're reading too much into it."

Rashid pointed down to the village. "Where is everybody?"

Sarcastically, Austin answered, "Maybe Ebola killed them all."

Rashid ignored the comment and instead cut a path through the bushy sweet potatoes, heading toward Isaac Luwum's whitewashed cinderblock house on the western edge of town.

Chapter 4

Isaac Luwum, their sponsor, maintained a hedge of unruly native plants around the edges of his front yard. Austin and Rashid hopped over the short hedge and tromped on the worn, patchy grass on their way to the open front door.

"Benoit? Margaux?" Austin called as he stepped into the main room. It was unusual for no one to be home. "Isaac?"

"I'll bet Isaac is drinking with that cabbage farmer." Rashid nodded toward the back of the house where Benoit and Margaux shared a room. "I'll bet I know what they're doing." Rashid stopped to listen.

"No. I don't hear anything." Austin crossed through the brightly painted, overly decorated living room, then glanced in the kitchen and through the windows on the back of the house. "She's usually pretty noisy. You'd know already if they were doing it."

"Maybe they're done and they went to sleep."

"Go knock on their door and see if they're in there." Austin went into the kitchen and poured some water from one of the jugs. He hollered, "We're almost out of water and it's your turn to boil."

"Nobody here," Rashid called, his voice notching a few tones higher as he walked toward the living room. He was getting anxious.

"This is weird." Austin crossed the living room again, tossed his backpack on the worn old couch, and dropped down beside it.

Rashid stood in the center of the living room and looked down at Austin. "Nobody is outside. Benoit and Margaux are gone—"

"They're not here." Austin shook his head slowly and took another drink. "That doesn't imply whatever you think you're implying when you say *gone*. Maybe they got tired of doing it in the bedroom and are off in the jungle, pretending they're horny monkeys or something."

"You don't think this is weird?" Rashid asked.

"You're letting your imagination convince you that something was wrong," said Austin. "You need to be cool, Rashid. It's dinnertime. Everybody is at home eating."

Rashid replied, "That's stupid. You know everybody doesn't go inside and eat at exactly the same time."

"I know. I'm just saying that you're getting worked up for no reason. It's like all the business you told me on the way here from Mbale about there being a billion people in Africa and only a couple thousand cases of Ebola in recorded history was just some bullshit you were telling yourself so that *you* wouldn't be scared." Austin grinned. "Are you worried about Ebola, Rashid? You can tell me."

"It's no wonder Najid doesn't like Americans."

"Your brother doesn't like us because we're smartasses?" Austin laughed. "Or is it because now that he suffers the burden of counting all your father's oil money he's pissed because we won't buy Priuses?"

"What are you talking about?"

"Nothing," said Austin. "Get a drink. Put your stuff on your bunk and we'll go out and see what's up. Cool?"

Rashid kicked a stray pillow to demonstrate his frustration and headed toward the room he shared with Austin.

Austin drank the rest of his water, stood up, and looked out at the street through the front window. Still, no one was out. It was weird. But he was sure there was an explanation.

It could be fear over the Ebola rumors. The army *had* blocked the road. That would be enough to frighten the people of any town.

Rashid came out of the room and went into the kitchen to get himself a cup of water. Some pots rattled as he looked for the kettle. "I could make some tea. Do you want any?"

"Up to you. You want to go out and find out what's going on first?"

Austin heard Rashid set the teakettle on the counter. Then he didn't hear anything. He looked back into the kitchen. Rashid's head was down. He wasn't moving. Austin asked, "Are you worried?"

"Najid called me yesterday. He says all he sees on the news are stories about Ebola. I told him not to worry. Ebola is in West Africa. We're in East Africa. But he kept telling me about all the hundreds of people who are dying and about how this is the worst outbreak ever."

Austin raised his hands in frustration. "You convinced me that the odds of us getting Ebola are so astronomically small that I shouldn't worry about it."

"That's the same thing I told Najid."

"But?"

"He worries. He told me to get on a plane and come home. He said he had a ticket waiting for me in Entebbe."

"When's the flight?"

"It was this morning. He said if I didn't get on that plane, he'd come here and grab me by the ear, put me on a plane, and take me home. His worries are infecting me, I think."

"Look, Rashid, I don't know much about Ebola. Somebody has to bleed on you or something. And I read it has a long incubation time."

"How do you know this?" Rashid asked.

"I did a little bit of research before I came over," said Austin. "I came across an underreported story about a small outbreak in Sierra Leone and that piqued my curiosity. Mostly what I wanted to know was what I could catch while I was here, and how I could avoid it."

"What are you telling me?"

Austin said, "We left the village last week. Six days ago. There was no Ebola here when we left. If by some really bad luck somebody caught it from a monkey or whatever, it would be, like, one person. That's it. There is no such thing as a whole village full of patient zeroes. So if somebody got it, their caregiver might get it, too. And so on, and so on. It could take a month or two before enough people get it for anybody but the local doctor to even notice."

Rashid didn't say anything.

Austin sat back down on the couch. "Take a deep breath. Make the tea. We'll drink some. Then we'll go. For all we know, Benoit and Margaux will come back while the water is coming to a boil and we can ask them what's going on. If not, we'll go over to the hospital and ask Dr. Littlefield. He'll know."

Chapter 5

At first, Salim hated Pakistan. Every single thing about it was unlike America. Of course, he expected that. But after living nineteen of his twenty years in a Denver suburb, and only one year in Hyderabad, the romantic *idea* of Pakistani life—the basis for his expectations—was nothing like the reality.

From the moment he landed in Lahore and walked off the plane, it started. The air was pungent with the smell of curry, diesel fumes, a whole range of plant smells, and even a bit of rotting garbage. All the smells of a city that one gets used to and doesn't even notice, until suddenly replaced by a whole different set of smells, becoming a constantly noticeable reminder of alien-ness.

But that was just the first thing.

The people spoke English with an accent that Salim had a hard time following. Of course, his parents spoke with a similar accent. However, they used good grammar in calm, slow, educated speech—not the rushed slang of people on the street.

Salim's accent was distinctly American, and that earned him suspicious glances from everyone he spoke to. His sense of alienation made the suspicion feel like hate. Back on that day, as he waited three hours for his tardy contact to come forward and collect him, he sulked near a ticket counter, trying to figure out how to turn his meager cash into a ticket back to Denver.

In fact, he'd been looking at his watch as he sat there, and had picked the top of the upcoming hour as the time when he'd stop waiting and call his father to beg him for money to buy that ticket. But ten minutes before the hand reached twelve on the clock face, a man walked up to him. "Salim?" he asked.

From there, Salim and his bag were hurried out of the airport, rushed into a taxi, and dropped off on a crowded street. He was hustled through block after block of pushing and shoving people, and finally trundled off in a rickety white van. Five others, silent young men with worried faces, shared the rear seats of the van with Salim. A driver and the man in charge sat in front.

They spent the better part of two days heading north in the van, slowly navigating roads which were mostly rutted paths, wide enough for the van but not much more. It was hot. It was dusty. It was a miserable trip. When one of the frightened young men tried to strike up a conversation to pass the time, he was scolded so fiercely that no one in the van attempted to speak for the rest of the trip.

On his second night in Pakistan, Salim and the other young men spent the night in a house that looked like the ones he'd seen on TV whenever soldiers were raiding villages in Afghanistan or drones were blowing them up in Pakistan. Pale stone walls with barren courtyards, the houses were all the sandy color of the surrounding dirt. And everywhere there were dirty, third-world people.

The six shared a room for the night: four on bunks, two on the floor. One of the brave among them whispered a question, and after that a quiet conversation grew. One of Salim's fellow travelers was from Canada, one from Florida. Two were from the UK, and another hailed from Germany. All were children of Muslim immigrants and had spent most—if not all—of their lives in their respective countries.

The next day, Salim was put in the back of a dilapidated Japanese pickup with Jalal, a nineteen-year-old from

London with a comically thick working-class English accent. They rode in the truck most of that day, along dirt roads that wound their way past mountain villages and a few towns. They whispered about where they might be — Pakistan or maybe Afghanistan. Though it could have been Tajikistan or China, for all they knew.

Late that day, with the temperatures dipping near freezing, they arrived at their new home and training center, a complex of buildings that looked to have grown up out of the dirt. Indoor plumbing was a luxury left hundreds, if not thousands of miles behind. Comfortable, bug-free mattresses were replaced with cots made of blankets over sticks lashed together. The kitchen was an outdoor cook's fire. It was camping, only instead of a tent Salim slept between stone walls under a leaky roof.

Chapter 6

Two months in, Salim had gotten used to the thin air, the cold nights, the simple meals, and Spartan life. They trained six days a week, usually four at a time under their two instructors on marksmanship, ambush, shooting from a moving vehicle, physical conditioning, and a host of other skills that any good jihadist might need.

With six trainees in the camp, two would take the rotating duty of drone watch while the other four trained. Keeping out of sight when drones were overhead kept them out of the crosshairs when America's politicians needed to boost their popularity with news feeds of exploding Muslims.

Salim scanned the sky. "I hate watching for drones."

"It's an easy day." Jalal handed the binoculars to Salim, "It's your turn."

Salim lifted them to his eyes and looked at several high, wispy clouds off to the west, thinking that maybe he saw a bright spot up there. "Has anyone ever seen a drone?"

"Dhakwan saw one last week," said Jalal. "You knew that. I was there when he told you."

"He saw something," said Salim, finding himself asking why every single thing said by anybody needed to be taken on faith.

"It was a drone."

"How do you know it wasn't a passenger jet or something else?" Salim asked.

Jalal pointed to the south. "Dhakwan said it was in the sky that way. They say there are five or six camps near the base of that mountain."

"We're not supposed to know where the other camps

are." Salim shook his head and looked at the mountain, curiosity making him wonder if he could see the camps.

Jalal chuckled. "If the CIA catches me and tortures me what will I tell them? The camps are at the base of a mountain? Which mountain, they'd ask. What could I say? I still don't know where we are."

Salim said, "You better learn something to tell them when they torture you because you know they won't stop until you do."

"I know as much as you," Jalal said, "which is nothing."

They both laughed and didn't worry about being scolded for it. A few hundred meters to the east of the compound, the two instructors and the trainees were sitting in the back of an SUV with the rear door open, shooting at targets nailed to trees and making too much noise.

Jalal said, "The only thing we see besides mountains and sky are the other trainees and our instructors. We don't even know their real names."

"Be thankful you don't."

"We see the truck that brought us here driven by a no-name man with a beard, dressed like every other peasant we saw on the road. He comes now and again. He drops off food and sometimes ammunition. That's everything I know."

Salim looked at another far away spot in the sky. It turned out to be a bird. "Do you think we'll get killed by a drone in our sleep one day?"

"Does it matter how we die as long as it's not running away like a coward?"

"I suppose not," Salim mused.

"It only matters that we die for jihad, to stop things like this." Jalal pointed at the sky. "I don't know what you heard in America—your news is little better than propaganda—but drones kill more innocents than combatants."

"We hear about some of that on the news." Salim lowered the binoculars. Holding them up too long made his arms tired. "That's one of the reasons I'm here."

"It's the *main* reason I'm here. Rich countries think they can murder Muslims who have no money, and nobody will care. It's wrong."

Salim nodded and the two sat in silence for a long time after that, scanning the sky both with and without the binoculars.

"What do you think we'll do?" Jalal asked.

Salim shrugged. "We spend a lot of time training with the RPGs."

"I hope it's not a bomb vest. I don't mind dying, but I want to die fighting. The thought of blowing myself up to kill people is unsatisfying."

"Unsatisfying?" Salim gave Jalal a sidelong glance. "What does that mean?"

"I want to see the results of my work, at least some of it," answered Jalal. "If you wear a vest, you press a button, and then you're in heaven. You don't even feel pain. You're just gone."

"You want to see Americans die before you go?" Salim asked.

"Americans? Brits? Any Westerner? No, I'd be happier to kill soldiers, but it doesn't matter. In those democracies—if you can call them that—people vote for governments that kill Muslims. They buy the bombs with their taxes, sit their fat asses on their couches, suck in all the Muslim hate propaganda, and tell themselves because they have no uniform on they have no guilt. But they are *all* guilty."

"Be careful, Jalal. You're starting to sound like a zealot."

Jalal laughed. "If we're not both zealots, what are we doing here?"

"Sometimes I wonder."

"Don't say that to anybody else." Jalal looked around. "You hear me, mate?"

"Yeah." Salim handed the binoculars back to Jalal.

"Dhakwan says his cousin was put in a sleeper cell in Germany. He thinks they're building a network and when the time is right, we'll take our RPGs to every major airport in the West, sit at the end of the runways, and shoot down airliners until they stop flying."

"That's stupid."

Jalal turned and raised his voice. "Stupid?"

"Calm down, Jalal. That won't work."

"Why won't it work, Mr. Weapons Expert?"

Salim said, "You've used the RPG. Tell me, what is the range of that weapon?"

"A few hundred meters," answered Jalal.

"Right."

Salim asked, "How high is a plane flying when it gets to the end of the runway?"

"Thirty meters. A hundred meters. It depends on the airport."

"And how close can you get to the end of the runway?" Salim asked.

"Depends, I guess," answered Jalal.

Salim kept pushing, "How fast is an airliner moving at the end of the runway?"

"A hundred and fifty miles per hour? More?"

Salim nodded. "Probably what I'd guess. And accelerating. How fast does your RPG round fly?"

"I don't know." Jalal shrugged, frowning.

"I don't either," said Salim. "Is it as fast as a bullet?"

"No, of course not. They don't tell us these things. You know that. It's not important for us to know."

"Is it as fast as a car?" Salim asked.

"Faster."

"Is it as fast as an airplane?"

Jalal's face grew thoughtful.

"You can see the round accelerate," said Salim. "You can see it all the way to the target."

"And?"

"I don't know how fast the RPG flies, but I'll bet a plane flies faster."

"That doesn't matter." Jalal sounded defiant.

"Why?"

"If we're at the end of the runway, we simply shoot the plane as it's coming toward us."

"And if you hit it—and that's a big if—where will the wreckage fall?" Salim asked.

Jalal shrugged.

"I don't know either." Salim shook his head. "But I guess some would probably land on you."

"I'll shoot when its overhead."

Salim suppressed a laugh. "So on your very first attempt, you're going to hit an airplane that's a hundred meters over your head, traveling at two hundred miles an hour away from you with an RPG round that might be going slower than the plane. And on your first attempt, you're going to guess how to lead the plane by just the right amount? Is that right?"

Jalal fell silent again.

"How would we train for that?" Salim asked. "I mean if they wanted that kind of attack to succeed, wouldn't we train for that?"

Jalal's voice faltered as he said, "You're my only friend here, Salim, but sometimes you make me feel stupid."

Salim laughed out loud, then looked around to make sure the instructors weren't in sight. "I'm not that smart, Jalal. I used to hang out with a bunch of guys in school that made me feel stupid all the time. Not on purpose, but they always talked about computer programming and their calculus homework and stuff. I just felt stupid by being around them, but they were my friends."

Jalal nodded for no real reason.

"I'm not trying to make you feel stupid." Salim turned to face Jalal. "Just *think*, that's all. Dhakwan believes things because he *wants* to believe them, not because they are based on any kind of fact. I'm not that smart, but I'm smart enough to know to ask questions. And sometimes all you have to do is ask questions and things that aren't true fall apart under examination. That's all."

Jalal nodded again, "That's good advice, Salim. "

Salim pointed to a spot overhead. Jalal examined the blue sky with the binoculars.

"Do you miss anything about America?" Jalal asked.

Salim thought about it for a minute, but had trouble gleaning down his long list to something that sounded worthy of being missed. "Do you miss anything about London?"

"Some." Jalal sighed. "Coming here, is this what you thought it would be?"

Salim shook his head, but wasn't sure what to say.

Chapter 7

Kapchorwa's few hundred shanties, houses, buildings, and huts surrounded a particularly snaky section of red dirt road on the lower northern slopes of Mt. Elgon. The road straightened out east of town and didn't hit any sizable population center until it was well into Kenya.

Behind the town to the south, Mt. Elgon, wrapped in misty forests and shades of green, rose to fourteen thousand feet. Up there, locals farmed coffee or worked at one of the resorts that catered to tourists anxious to hike the mountain and stand under Sipi Falls. To the northeast, more mountains grew up out of the fertile plains dotted with farms and forest. Far below to the west, the flat land stretched until all the details faded to a gray that was consumed by a sky blazing yellow and orange in the setting sun.

Austin always stopped for at least a moment to watch the sun set in the evenings. It was a wholly different experience than what he was used to back home in Denver —being on the plain, watching the sun sink behind the Rocky Mountains.

"Let's go."

Austin turned away from the yellow sky, took a few quick steps to catch up with Rashid, and together they walked up the center of the dirt road through the deserted town. An occasional muffled cry carried on the wind. Austin cocked his head to try to hear it again, but the sounds were elusive and soft, hard to define.

Ahead on the hospital's wide front porch, a heavyset figure was reaching up to put a flame in the lantern that hung above the door.

"Electricity is out again," Rashid deduced.

With the lantern's glow growing, the woman went back inside.

Austin said, "That was Nurse Mary-Margaret, I think."

"Yeah," Rashid agreed.

They continued up the road, seeing no one until they climbed the six steps up to the hospital's porch and let themselves in the front door. The smell of sickness rolled out of the interior gloom, turning Austin's stomach.

Lanterns hanging down the length of the ward on the ceiling's beams weren't bright enough to lift the rectangular room entirely out of darkness. The concrete floor reflected little light, and the sea foam green paint on the lower half of the cinderblock walls didn't help. A dozen screened windows were equally spaced across the white upper half of each of the walls. Those on the west side of the building let in the last of the sun's rays.

At the other end of the ward, one door opened to a simple operating room, another to an exam room, and a supply closet. The two shabby desks that usually sat just inside and on either side of the door were gone. Not moved to anywhere Austin could see — they were just gone. Near the far end, Dr. Littlefield, an American, was talking to his Ugandan counterpart, Dr. Ruhindi. Nurse Mary-Margaret had just joined them. The two African nurses, faces covered with surgical masks, full aprons, and rubber gloves, were each busy doing something for one of the —

Austin's mouth fell open as his eyes adjusted to the dimness and he saw the number of patients.

With forty-eight generously spaced beds, the hospital hadn't been more than half full all summer. But extra cots had been brought in, all of which were full. Even the space between the beds was covered in rows of people lying on mats and blankets, sleeping, coughing, and bleeding. The smell of urine, feces, and vomit were thick in the air. Austin covered his mouth.

Some primal memory told him those people were dying, while instinct urged him to run.

The door banged closed. Nurse Mary-Margaret turned and hurried toward them. The look on her face made it clear that it had been a mistake for them to come inside.

Chapter 8

Austin couldn't take his eyes off of the hundred people lying on soiled sheets as they coughed and wheezed and stared into space with all hope gone from their eyes. Nurse Mary-Margaret bodily pushed him and Rashid out onto the front porch, pulling the door closed behind her. "Why did you come back?"

"Uh," was all Austin could think to say, feeling like he'd been punched in the gut.

In a voice that seemed to come from somewhere down the street, Rashid asked, "Ebola?"

Nurse Mary-Margaret nodded and tears welled up in her eyes, but they didn't flow. She had gotten very good at keeping them under control. "You should go to your sponsor's house. Stay there."

"Nobody's home," Austin said, as though that had any relevance. He was still reeling.

Mary-Margaret glanced over her shoulder at the closed door behind her.

"What?" Austin implored. There was something in that look.

Rashid asked, "Isaac…is he in there?"

For a second, Mary-Margaret didn't answer. "Yes."

Austin started putting the pieces together. "Benoit, Margaux. They're not at the house."

Mary-Margaret hesitated again. "Inside."

"They have Ebola?"

Mary-Margaret shook her head but said, "Yes."

Rashid asked, "Will they die?"

Nurse Mary-Margaret didn't nod, she didn't shake her

head. She seemed stuck between the two gestures.

"That doesn't answer the question." Rashid was afraid. Whether for himself or the others, Austin couldn't tell.

"There is no answer," Mary-Margaret said.

The three looked at one another in silence, each waiting for one of the others to lead. Austin didn't know what to do. Going back to the house, drinking—again—from the same water, the same cups, using the same utensils that Isaac, Benoit, and Margaux had used, would put him and Rashid at risk.

In many ways, it wasn't a risk. If the Ebola virus was in the house, Austin feared they already had it. "I've heard that it's transmitted by bodily fluids. What other ways can we catch it?" Austin looked at Rashid. "We may already be infected."

"Why do you say that?" Mary-Margaret feigned doubt, but it was a thin, pointless mask.

Austin explained that they drank water when they got back to the house.

"There's nothing certain about that." Nurse Mary-Margaret shook her head. "Direct contact with the bodily fluids of something or someone who is infected is the only way we know for sure to contract Ebola. You're probably not infected. Dump the water and boil everything when you get back to the house."

"How did Isaac, Benoit, and Margaux get infected?" Austin asked.

"They were helping with the other patients. They've been here since it started."

"When did it start?" Austin didn't remember anything unusual in Kapchorwa when they left nearly a week earlier. Had the disease been present and he didn't notice?

"The day after you left for Mbale."

"How long does it take for the symptoms to show up after you've been exposed?"

"A few days to several weeks," answered Mary-Margaret.

Austin gestured at Rashid. "So me and Rashid could already have it. We could have caught it before we left."

Mary-Margaret asked, "What are you saying, Austin? You want to have this disease?"

"No. Definitely not. But if these people started showing symptoms the day after we left for Mbale, they were exposed well before that, while me and Rashid were still here. We may have been infected then, and are just not symptomatic yet. Right?"

Mary-Margaret nodded. "Just go home."

Austin looked back down the street to see the remains of the sunset colors in the western sky, realizing that he was buying time while he searched for a decision.

Full of idealism, he'd wrangled his way into a program that sent college kids to Africa to help. And the goal was that general, to help. When he volunteered he said he was open to anything. He wanted to do his small part to make the world a better place. So, in a country where parents are charged tuition to send their kids to any level of school, Austin was assigned to teach street kids — kids who otherwise had zero chance at an education — for free.

But now he was standing on the front porch of a dramatically understaffed hospital full of diseased patients who needed help if they were to have any chance at survival. Even his students were either inside or they had already fled. With quite possibly the same virus swimming in his veins, attacking and bursting his cells, Austin needed to decide if he was going to cower in his dying sponsor's house, or put his life at real risk to help.

He needed to decide if his convictions ran deep or if he was just a tourist wearing a humanitarian disguise, looking for the most unique pictures to post on his Facebook page. In a shaky voice, Austin replied, "I'm volunteering to help in the hospital."

Rashid said, "You're taking away my options with your foolish bravery."

Austin looked at Rashid. "You don't have to. Go home. Be safe."

"No." Rashid hesitated an awkwardly long time, before he finally managed to say, "I want to help."

"Rashid, you're only here because your father wants you to learn about life in the *real* world."

Rashid put on a brave face. "I've learned enough. I'll help."

Mary-Margaret shook her head. "You boys are fools."

Austin looked at Rashid then back at the nurse. "What do you want us to do?"

"I want you to go home and sleep. Talk about what you think you're doing, and keep reminding each other that you could be dead in two weeks if you do this. Come see me in the morning if you still want to help."

Chapter 9

Austin woke when the nightmare of a pygmy pounding on his skull with a hammer became too painful to be just a dream. He sat up in his bed and every part of his body ached. The room was hot. The barest sliver of early morning light came in through the window.

He put his hands to his temples and groaned. Nearly stumbling as he got up, he knelt down beside the bed and pulled his bag out from underneath. He let his face fall on the mattress under the weight of a wave of pain behind his eyes, a throbbing strong enough to take his breath away.

"Jesus Christ, that *hurts*."

He found a bottle, made out the aspirin label, and struggled with the childproof cap. Another hammer of pain interrupted the effort. He turned and sat on the cool floor, turned his attention back to the contrary little cap, and managed to remove it. He took out four aspirin and put them in his mouth, knowing he had no water. He and Rashid hadn't boiled anything the night before and he couldn't bring himself to drink anything still in the house.

He chewed and grimaced at the bitterness, telling himself over and over again that the taste wasn't as bad as tequila. He was unable to swallow. His mouth was too dry.

He chewed and chewed, grinding the bitter pills to powder, then mud, as he slowly generated some saliva.

Up on his knees again, Austin propped himself on the bed and rested before standing. Moisture was working its way into his mouth. He chewed some more, managed to swallow the aspirin's crumbs and decided that standing at just that moment was a bad idea. He eased himself down onto the hard floor, then laid his belly, his chest, and face on the cold tile, and closed his eyes.

After a while, his breathing stabilized, his head pounded less, and he tried to think of what he'd drunk to give himself such a monster hangover. The fragments of memory slowly fell into place in his mind. He was in Mbale. He'd ridden on the back of a boda for hours. The deserted town. The hospital.

"Crap."

Austin reached up and put a hand on his forehead. He felt hot.

"Crap."

He sat up and leaned back against his bed. Across the room, Rashid was sleeping on his narrow bed, on his belly with an arm dangling over the side. His hand lay on the floor by a puddle of his last meal, spilled from his stomach.

"Oh, no."

Despite the headache, Austin sprang across the room and shook Rashid's shoulder with one hand as he put the tips of his fingers on Rashid's jugular, feeling for a pulse. Rashid was alive. At least he hadn't choked to death in his sleep. But his skin was on fire. Austin rolled him onto his back. Reeking vomit was all over Rashid's face, down his chest, and on the thin mattress.

"Oh, shit. Oh, shit." He shook Rashid again. "Wake up. Wake up."

Rashid didn't respond.

Austin shook again. "Rashid!"

Nothing.

Austin heaved a few deep breaths. He had to get Rashid to the hospital. The specter of Ebola and bodily fluids screamed at him to step away, but in that moment it didn't matter. Anyone too sick to wake up was too sick to be at home. He needed a doctor. Austin pushed his arms under Rashid and with all the effort he could muster, he hauled Rashid up.

Chapter 10

Kapchorwa. In the local language, it meant "friendly people." And they were. Big-hearted, smiling people.

Were.

Thinking about that and starting to feel hopeless, Dr. Littlefield sat on the porch of the hospital and leaned against the wall, feeling stomped on by an extreme lack of sleep. During the night, Dr. Ruhindi fell out of the ranks of caregivers and into the ranks of the patients. The virus hit him hard and fast. Dr. Littlefield suspected that he'd been sick for at least a few days and was hiding the symptoms, just as he knew one of the African nurses was. Just like anyone else, Dr. Ruhindi could only push a sick body so far on willpower. He collapsed late in the night, and by the time the sun was rising, he was barely able to hold himself up on his hands and knees to puke into the bucket by his bed.

Dr. Littlefield looked up the road, hoping to see a medical convoy. It was a hope that was dashed each time he left the ward to take some time to breathe fresh air and rest his bones on the porch.

He wondered what happened to the blood samples he'd sent through Mbale and on to Kampala. The man charged with the task never returned. At the time Littlefield had sent the samples, he didn't know if the nightmare that crawled up out of the jungle slime and attacked the poor, ignorant farmers of Kapchorwa was Ebola. He suspected it, but told himself for at least a few reasons that it couldn't be that particular virus.

Ebola, that little bastard of a bug, had popped up earlier in the summer in Sierra Leone in the worst outbreak in history. Was it possible that global warming had changed something important about the ecological balance in Africa and turned it into an optimal, continent-sized petri dish for breeding that virus?

No.

As much as Dr. Littlefield liked to toy with that suspicion, he knew in his heart that a catastrophic Ebola epidemic in Africa was inevitable. With advances in medicine and farming, the population density in Africa had tripled in the past sixty years. Now there were three times as many poverty-stricken people in large swaths of the continent, with a culture and living conditions seemingly designed to increase the body count during disease outbreaks.

And as far as the outbreak in Kapchorwa, it was likely the case that some local native had been working in Sierra Leone and had quietly fled when the disease took root there, unwittingly bringing the Ebola home with him.

Littlefield looked across the rusty roofs of the houses spread down Mt. Elgon's slope as the sun slowly rose over them. He wondered in which of those houses the plague carrier lay—if not dead already—in the final stages of the disease. He knew that the plague carrier couldn't be among those dying in the hospital behind him. He knew most of those by name or by sight. None of them had been in Sierra Leone.

But in all of that, the thing that just didn't make any sense was how fast the disease had taken hold in the small population of Kapchorwa. How could any disease transmitted through bodily fluids have spread so quickly, infecting so many in such a short time? It didn't make any sense at all.

Perhaps there was some secret ritual peculiar to these

people that helped spread the disease with such comprehensive rapidity.

Or, it was airborne. In that case, a single carrier could infect a few or maybe a dozen, and those people would infect others, and the process would domino across the small farming community in no time. Ironically, the only thing that gave Dr. Littlefield hope was the chance that the disease wasn't Ebola but some kind of particularly contagious flu. Kapchorwa lay in the tropics after all. Who knew how many nasty bugs lingered under the bushes and in the local monkeys' blood?

And no one in the village had yet bled out and died.

With no deaths as of yet, Dr. Littlefield had to reconsider how he'd arrived at the conclusion that Kapchorwa's little epidemic was Ebola. Was it just fear of the disease, due to the outbreak in West Africa that put the thought in his mind? Possibly. The symptoms were consistent with Ebola so far: raging headache, fever, nausea, diarrhea, red eyes, rash, unexplained bruising, but no external hemorrhaging —not yet. Had the roadblocks set up by an overreacting Ugandan government influenced his diagnosis? *Possibly.*

Perhaps his Ebola fears were just that—fears.

Dr. Littlefield told himself that he was not a fearful man, not a reactionary.

Movement down the street caught Dr. Littlefield's eye. He looked up. His heart sank. A guy—that kid who was teaching the street children for the summer—was carrying someone else up the center of the deserted road. The day's count of new infections was starting early.

Chapter 11

In the hospital's exam room, Austin looked out through the open door of the ward as the sun shown in through the east-facing windows. He lifted Rashid's satellite phone and dialed Najid Almasi, Rashid's older brother. On the third ring, someone answered.

"Hello?" said Austin.

A terse voice said something in Arabic.

"Hello? Do you speak English?" asked Austin.

The irritated voice said, "Who is this?"

"Austin Cooper. I'm a friend of Rashid."

"You are American."

"Yes."

"Why are you calling me on Rashid's telephone?"

"Is this Najid Almasi?"

"I'll ask again. Why do you have this telephone?"

Austin was reluctant to divulge his information without knowing whether the person on the other end was Najid or not. But what choice did he have? "I don't know how much you know about what Rashid is doing in Uganda, but I am his roommate. We work together with the street kids."

A long pause followed before the voice said, "You are the one he talked about."

"Yes. I'm Austin."

The voice repeated, "Austin."

"Yes. If you are not Rashid's brother, Najid, I need to speak with him. Please, it's important."

"Has something happened to Rashid?"

"He's sick."

There was a silence that lasted for a long time. That was

to be expected. Sick could have many meanings—many deadly ones—with Ebola on the loose.

"Can he talk?"

"Not right now. He's not conscious."

"What does that mean?"

"He had a fever when I found him this morning. He wouldn't wake up."

Another silence.

"You are in Kapchorwa?" asked Najid.

"Yes, in the hospital there."

"I will be there in six hours."

"What? How?"

"That is no concern of yours. It would be a great favor to me if you saw to my brother's care until I arrive."

"Um." Six hours? Najid must have been on his way already. "Of course."

Chapter 12

"Dr. Littlefield thinks it might be typhoid." Nurse Mary-Margaret led Austin into the exam room, then stopped in front of a wide stainless steel sink. "Wash. Use that soap and plenty of it. See that poster above the sink?"

Austin nodded at the poster. "You mean this one that tells me how to wash my hands?"

"Yes. Follow the directions exactly. Just because you've washed your hands a million times since you were little doesn't mean you've ever done it correctly."

"Yes, ma'am." Austin asked, "If it's typhoid, it would be in the water, right?"

"We have our own cistern. We only use well water as a last resort."

Austin leaned over the sink and turned on the faucet.

Nurse Mary-Margaret pushed a thermometer into Austin's mouth. "I know you think you feel good enough to help, but if your temperature is too high, you need to be in a cot."

"A cot?" Austin tried to smile. They both knew there were no cots available, nor places to put them.

"A pallet on the floor, then. Keep your mouth shut, so I can get a temperature."

Austin scrubbed his hands and arms up to his elbows, and then raised them to let them dry as he'd seen doctors do on TV.

Nurse Mary-Margaret hung a blue apron over his head and turned him around to tie it. "Let's hope this is typhoid. Thieves stole most of our supplies the day after the outbreak started here."

"You're shitting me."

"I'm not." Nurse Mary-Margaret took the thermometer out of Austin's mouth and looked at it with a frown. Without looking up, she asked, "And how do you feel?"

Austin figured it would be best not to mention the four aspirin he'd taken an hour earlier. "I'll live."

Nurse Mary-Margaret shook her head and directed her frown at him instead of the thermometer. "Those figures of speech are funny when you miss a day of school back in Detroit or wherever you're from —"

"Denver."

" — but they mean something real here. You should know that now."

Austin accepted the scolding without comment. She was right. "I don't feel good, but I feel good enough to help in the ward. If I get too sick, I'll let you know and take a spot on the floor."

She put a surgical mask to his face and hooked the elastic bands over his ears. "Don't take this off. We don't know for sure yet that you're sick with what they've got, and if you are, we don't want you infecting anyone who isn't."

"Yes, ma'am."

She instructed him on the complex process of putting on surgical gloves. After that, Nurse Mary-Margaret put her hands on Austin's shoulder and held him in front of her, demanding one hundred percent of his attention. "You need to understand, Austin, if this *is* Ebola, odds are — with what little protection we still have to put on — you'll catch it and you'll die. Most do."

Austin nodded.

"I know you think you have whatever everybody else has, but you don't know that. If you don't, and you come in here to help with this inadequate protection, you'll get what they've got."

"But it could be typhoid."

"Don't do that. You know that hope is as thin as I know it is. Ebola is sixty to ninety percent deadly. You're young and healthy, so that may increase your odds of survival, but if you walk into that ward, it may be the decision that costs you your life."

"*You're* helping," he replied.

Mary-Margaret huffed. "This has nothing to do with me. I've already had a good, long life. I have sons older than you. I have grandchildren."

"If I go in, will I be helpful? Will it give some of those people a chance to live? Or will I be wasting my time?"

"You'll be helpful. There aren't enough of us to help these people already, and if more come today, we'll be overwhelmed."

"Is there any help on the way?" Austin asked.

She smiled weakly. "We sent word to Kampala, and we're praying."

"What about the short-wave radio?"

"The radio man is down with the disease. He can barely remember his own name."

Austin looked off in the direction he'd seen the shortwave radio antenna attached to a building in town. "I think—"

Mary-Margaret shook her head. "The real world isn't like a Gilligan's Island episode, Austin Cooper. Operating a shortwave radio isn't as easy as flipping a switch. It's not a telephone."

Chapter 13

With a tremendous effort, Margaux propped herself up on one elbow, held the position for a moment, and fell back on her pillow. "Oh, God."

From where he sat on her cot, Austin looked down at Rashid and Benoit on their blankets on the floor and asked Margaux, "How are you doing?"

In her French accent she said, "That's a *stupid* question."

"I know. I'm being polite."

"You shouldn't be in here," she told him.

"I know. I'm being polite."

Margaux started to laugh, but it turned into a painful cough, and she rolled onto her side. "I feel like I'm dying."

Austin put a gloved hand on her shoulder. "You'll be okay."

"That doesn't mean anything coming from you."

"Not medically." Austin looked around the stinking ward. There was barely room to walk. The influx of patients throughout the day had filled most of the space. "It's what people say to sick people."

"Why?"

"You know why," he answered. "It means I've nothing meaningful to say, but I hope you get better."

"Why not say *that*?"

"I hope you get better. When you're sick, you're kind of a bitch." Austin smiled behind his mask.

Margaux smiled back. "I know. I'm sorry."

Austin noticed reddish splotches on her face and arms.

"Is Benoit awake?" Margaux asked.

"He was up earlier."

"Out of bed?"

Austin pointed at the door in the back of the ward. "I helped him to the outhouse."

"Good. I'm glad he was up."

"Yeah." In truth, Benoit had barely made it. Austin had half carried him on the way back, but didn't recall seeing a rash on Benoit's skin at the time. Looking down at Benoit from his position on Margaux's cot, Austin saw it now.

He'd seen those same splotches on the skin of others in the ward — others who were much worse off the Benoit or Margaux. They'd regurgitate and soil themselves and lie in their excretions. Half delirious, too fatigued, or in too much pain to do anything about it or even ask for help.

Once Nurse Mary-Margaret had put him to work, he started by helping to change the bed sheets under a young woman, one of the first to arrive, down at the end of the ward. She seemed to have lost all control of her bodily functions. Her temperature had set her blotched skin afire. Her blood-filled eyes rolled around, unable to focus on anything. Her vomitus was bloody and black. Her gums and nose wouldn't stop bleeding. She moaned whenever touched.

Austin didn't know much about death, but he was sure that girl was dying.

Heavy slow breathing from Margaux told Austin that she had fallen asleep.

"Hey." It was Rashid.

Austin looked down at Rashid and grinned behind his mask. "I thought you were dead."

"Is — is this the hospital?"

"Yeah." Rashid drew in a long, painful sounding breath. "I feel terrible."

"Yeah. You look like shit, too."

"I'm thirsty."

Austin stood up a little too fast and felt light-headed. It was time for more aspirin. "I'll get you some water."

A couple of large white plastic barrels were on tables against one wall. They'd been brought in a few hours earlier along with a case of disposable cups. The disposable cups were a good thought, but unless there were lots more somewhere close by, they'd run out before the end of the day.

Austin filled a cup and brought it to Rashid, who drank slowly at first and then gulped.

"Thank you," said Rashid.

"I'll get you some more in a minute."

"How did I get here?" Rashid asked.

"I carried you," answered Austin. "You wouldn't wake up this morning."

"So it was this morning. I was almost worried that I'd been out for a week or something."

Benoit squirmed, but didn't wake up.

Austin said, "No. Just today."

Rashid reached down and felt his pocket.

Austin said, "I took your phone and called your brother, Najid. At least I think it was him. How many brothers do you have?"

"Just Najid."

"Okay," said Austin. "He'll be here in a while."

"He shouldn't come."

"I know." Austin shrugged. "Tell *him* that."

"I will. Where is my phone?"

Austin leaned over Rashid and fetched the phone. It was

lying on the floor above Rashid's head.

Rashid didn't raise his hand to take the phone from Austin, but instead stared up at Austin for a few long moments. "Is it Ebola?"

"They're not sure. Nurse Mary-Margaret said it might be typhoid."

"That's great."

Austin chuckled. "Yeah, that's what I thought. I'll bet you never thought you'd be happy to have typhoid."

"So they're sure, then?"

Austin shook his head. "They don't know yet. They think because so many people got sick so fast, it can't be Ebola."

"Why don't they test?"

"I don't know. Maybe they did but the results aren't back yet."

Chapter 14

Paul Cooper wasn't the worrying type, not even close to it. Neither did he wear rose-colored glasses. He saw himself as a pragmatist. But one worry that did lurk in his little closet of childhood bogeymen was Ebola. He was a kid with a paper route when the 1976 outbreak hit the news. Every day when he folded his papers prior to delivering them on his bike, he read the headlines. He saw frightening stories of bleeding, suffering, and of whole African villages wiped out. And an American media, in the infancy of its sensationalist tendencies, taught him a new phrase for fear —hemorrhagic fever.

In those days, nobody knew what caused Ebola. Nobody knew how it was transmitted. There was speculation about something in the water or the air—an old contagious evil that had been hiding in the jungle's damp shadows, awakened.

Paul clearly remembered sitting on the living room floor one evening while his parents and grandparents watched the TV with silent mouths and wide eyes. Ebola was the kind of disease that scared the shit out of everybody.

But Africa was a far away place in those days. The deepest jungles of Zaire were even further away. For a disease that killed *everybody*, there seemed no way it could make its way out of the jungle in a jeep on a rutted dirt road, onto some bush pilot's little plane, onto a commercial flight to Europe, and eventually to America. The world wasn't as thoroughly interconnected by jets in those days as it was going to become. Anyone unlucky enough to be carrying the Ebola virus in his blood was likely never to make it out of the jungle alive.

Forty years later, things were different. Anyone sitting in

a thatch-roofed African hut infested with Ebola could make his way out of the jungle and onto an airplane that would drop him in any of America's busiest airports within twenty-four hours.

As paperboys do, Paul eventually finished school. He went to college, married, had kids of his own, and eventually got divorced; a regular kid who grew into a regular American life. As life passed, that scary disease's name came up occasionally in the news, and just like that other scary word from his childhood—thermonuclear war —it always caught his attention and tugged at his fears.

So when the Ebola outbreak came up in the news that summer, Paul was aware and felt a little remiss. The disease had been spreading from Sierra Leone to Guinea and Liberia—West African countries—for months before enough people had died to make it newsworthy. By then, it was the largest Ebola outbreak on record.

The kicker was that Austin, Paul's son, was already in Uganda for the summer.

Paul had been passively fretting over the stories out of Africa for weeks, thinking about his son near some little town named Mbale, close to the Kenyan border. Paul searched his usual news websites for information. He surfed sites he'd never heard of, groping for headlines. He researched the disease on Wikipedia to fill the gaps in his media-based knowledge of the disease. Through the process, his worry grew.

He checked a map program for the distance between Monrovia, the capital of Liberia, and Kampala, the capital of Uganda. He sat back in his chair, astounded. A little relieved, but astounded.

The distance from Los Angeles to New York in a country with arguably the best transportation infrastructure in the world was just under twenty-eight hundred miles. The distance from Monrovia to Kampala was over four thousand. He had never realized the tremendous scale of Africa.

How likely was it that anyone with the disease could get himself from Monrovia to Kampala, let alone Mbale, across thousands of miles of dirt roads—and a lot of them had to be dirt roads—or even by airplane? Paul decided that chance was small. Poor Africans weren't as mobile as affluent Americans and Europeans. Ebola was more likely to leap to London or New York than it was to Uganda.

And that gave Paul comfort. Austin was as safe from Ebola in Mbale as he was in Denver.

It was after the networks reported the story of two Ebola-infected doctors being flown from West Africa to Atlanta that Paul's concern ratcheted up again.

Bringing Ebola to America on purpose. What the fuck kind of craziness was that?

Paul put serious thought into driving down to the wholesale club and loading his truck with rice, beans, and peanut butter, or whatever the hell preppers stored in their basements. But he didn't. Instead, he vented his concerns in an evening of ranting on various Internet forums.

Now, Paul Cooper was sitting in his cubicle staring at a spreadsheet full of esoteric formulae when his phone chirped with an incoming text message. Heidi, with her own fears growing, told him that a traveler returning from West Africa had been hospitalized in New York and was being tested for Ebola.

"Shit."

Someone in the next cubicle said, "Huh?"

Paul didn't respond. He was thinking about what would

happen if the Ebola virus got a foothold in America.

He'd read enough about Ebola to know it spread through the transfer of bodily fluids or maybe just by skin touching skin. That was a big maybe to bet one's life on. He also read enough to know that the idiosyncrasies of many African cultures left them susceptible to the disease, as it wasn't uncommon for them to use their bare hands when tending to their sick or handling the dead.

He'd also seen a graph emailed to him by his daughter that showed the growth in the number of Ebola cases and the number of deaths. To Paul, it looked like an exponential curve. That curve made him afraid the West African outbreak might be due to an airborne strain of the virus. That, of course, flew in the face of what every single doctor or medical body said. Still, he had his fear, and fears aren't always rational.

One thing he did know, fear or not, was that an airborne strain of Ebola would devastate the world.

So with that fear in mind, he returned to one important question: what the hell do Doomsday Preppers keep in their basements, and how much of it would he need?

He'd seen magazine ads for post-apocalyptic meal kits, a kind of civilian version of MREs. They were really expensive, and would probably be impossible to get with Ebola epidemics in the news. Paul was sure every prepper in the country was topping off their own supplies.

But the problem wasn't that hard to figure out. People with a lot less education had been feeding themselves for millennia before Paul was born. The question became for how long would he need to prepare? A month? A year?

Would that really be necessary?

Paul closed the spreadsheets he'd been working on and

opened up a browser. He knew that in a pinch, he could get by on fifteen hundred calories a day. Twenty-five hundred would be better, but a few months on rations wouldn't be a bad way to lose those extra pounds that had accumulated around his waist over the decades. He searched for the number of calories in a pound of pinto beans, a pound of rice, and a pound of cooking oil.

A quick calculation told him that a fifty-pound bag of rice would be enough to keep him and Heidi on subsistence rations for three weeks. Not yummy—not by any means—but a fifty-pound bag of rice was cheap insurance. Throw in a fifty-pound bag of beans and maybe a five-gallon jug of cooking oil, add that to what was in the pantry on any given day, and he and Heidi would be good for three months on less than a hundred dollars. He'd dump the food in the back of the basement and it would keep forever—at least forever enough.

Extrapolating from there, four or five hundred dollars might be enough to keep them in boring food for a year. That left the problem of what to do about water. But those were thoughts for another day. One step at a time.

Paul got up from his desk. It was three o'clock. To hell with it. He crossed the aisle and leaned into his coworker's cubicle. "Hey, I'm heading out early."

"Okay."

Paul stepped back into his cubicle and packed up his laptop. Five minutes later, he was in his truck. Ten minutes after that, he was driving into a Costco parking lot, feeling frightened, self conscious, and silly all at the same time. But as silly as the whole exercise felt, he kept telling himself that a hundred bucks was a small price to pay to take the worry off his mind.

Chapter 15

A guy checked his membership card and rolled an enormous basket in front of him, wide enough to sit a few adults snuggly inside. Paul accepted the basket and pushed it down a long corridor of boxes stacked twice as tall as him, each with a ten-square-foot full-color picture of the flat panel television inside.

As Paul looked at the warehouse shelves, stacked forty feet high in rows past the flat panel gauntlet, he realized there was probably enough food in the building to keep him alive for the rest of his life. At the same time, he wondered — when society faltered under the strain of a real epidemic — whether looters coming to steal food would first grab a giant high-definition television or if they'd pick up a case of baby food instead. And those that carted a television out in one of these enormous baskets, would they do it because they were too stupid to take the food, or because they were too optimistic to think they'd need it?

Paul exited the flat panel cave and passed into a labyrinth of tables piled high with folded clothing. Once through that, he turned down the first of the food aisles looking for inexpensive calories. Instead, the aisle was full of snack crackers of every flavor imaginable, in boxes and plastic jugs each big enough to feed him and Heidi for a few days. But twenty dollars for two days' worth of snack crackers was a high price compared to a fifty-pound bag of rice that could feed them for three weeks.

Nevertheless, self-consciousness was setting in. He wanted the rice, beans, and oil, but he didn't want to look like an Ebola-fearing prepper, even if that was exactly what he was. So a giant-sized box of granola bars found its way into the basket. They were expensive calories, but a granola bar every other day would add a little variety to a diet of rice and beans. It would also be a distracting snack food when the cashier scrutinized his purchase. His feeling of silliness was setting in, and he was pretty sure the cashier was going to ask him why he needed food in such bulk.

He found the rice two aisles over. A fifty-pound bag of sugar made it into the basket—everything tastes good with sugar on it—along with a five-gallon jug of cooking oil. A double pack of large peanut butter jars joined all of that along with a gallon of honey, four pounds of salt, and a case of Cokes. No beans, though.

He made several circuits of the store looking for the beans. There were none to be found.

He picked up a jug of bleach, recalling from his Boy Scout days that a capful in some measure of water would render it drinkable. He didn't know if boiling would become necessary, or even doable. The bleach would give he and Heidi access to water sources that might otherwise be unusable.

Once in line at the cashier, his self-consciousness made him look around nervously, especially when he compared his load with the mixed greens, a bottle of wine, salmon, some fresh cut flowers, and a bag of apples being bought by the woman in front of him. She was planning on cooking a nice dinner and plying some guy with enough wine to make her wrinkles invisible so she could get him into bed.

The cashier rang up the woman and sent her on her way.

To Paul's relief, when his turn arrived to check out, neither the cashier nor her helper commented on his obvious Doomsday Prepper hoard. A few minutes later, the hoard was stashed in the back of his truck and he was driving home, wondering how he was going to explain fifty-pound bags of dry goods to Heidi.

Chapter 16

Getting the four-wheel drive vehicles undetected over the Ugandan border from Kenya was as easy as it was in any other part of the Third World. Najid Almasi and his men hadn't seen anything but shrubs, trees, animals, and farms since heading east across the road north of Kitale. They crossed the border far from any roads and far from any towns. No bribes needed to be paid.

More importantly, no questions needed to be asked. No witnesses needed to be paid extra to hold their tongues about eight armed Arab men who'd crossed the border — once into Uganda and once back out — with a sick young man riding along.

Having successfully crossed into Uganda on their way to Kapchorwa, they stopped their Land Rovers in the middle of the dirt road and they all got out.

One of the men took several boxes out of the back of Najid's Land Rover, opened them, and started passing out plastic-wrapped packets. Each of the eight men received one yellow Tyvek suit, a pair of elbow-length rubber gloves, goggles, a chemical protective hood, and a surgical mask. The men donned the gear. It was hot, suffocating equipment in the humid East African sun, but it was necessary, given the dangers ahead. They loaded back into the vehicles, and with air conditioners running at maximum, they drove the last few miles into Kapchorwa.

Chapter 17

They sat in a booth at the restaurant, because they *always* sat in a booth — usually the same booth. They ordered their usual pizza from their usual waiter, Nick. And as usual, Paul felt a pang of guilt because they spent too much money eating out. The evidence being that they had a usual booth, a usual pizza, and a usual waiter.

Heidi started checking her Facebook page on her phone as soon as Nick left the drinks. She checked in at the pizza place, checked the newsfeed, and wrote a comment about something that made her laugh to herself.

Paul swirled the ice in his glass with the straw and when the cubes had jingled against the glass enough times, he said, "You might think this is a little weird."

"What?" Heidi didn't look up from her phone, which wasn't unusual. She liked to tell herself that she was a multitasker, when in fact she was just good at lying to herself about ignoring people.

Paul was used to it. "After that story on the news yesterday I went to Costco and bought some stuff."

"Uh-huh." Heidi slid her finger down the screen, glanced up, smiled, and looked back down at her phone.

"I bought a fifty-pound bag of rice, five gallons of cooking oil, and some other stuff."

Heidi scrolled again, read some more, stopped, then looked up. "You what?"

"It's probably nothing. I mean, I may be worried about nothing, but after that story in the news about that guy showing up in New York with Ebola, I got worried."

"You think Ebola is here?" she asked.

"I honestly doubt it."

"What does this have to do with buying fifty pounds of rice at Costco?"

Paul looked around to assure himself that no one was listening to the conversation. "I'm a little embarrassed about it."

Heidi put her phone down on the table. She was ready to give her full attention.

Knowing that wouldn't last long, Paul continued, "I kind of feel like a prepper."

"A prepper?"

"You know. Like those Doomsday Preppers you see on TV."

She cringed. "You bought rice because you're a Doomsday Prepper?"

"No, not really. Maybe a little. Like I said, I got worried because of that Ebola thing in New York. If there's an outbreak there, things could kind of go to shit pretty quickly in the rest of the country. I just figured if I spent a hundred bucks or so at Costco, we'd be safe. In theory, we'd have enough to eat for two or three months in case we couldn't go out."

"*Rice*?" Heidi's tone made it clear she was displeased. "Please don't tell me it's white rice."

"They only had white in bulk. I couldn't find any brown."

"Bland, boring *white* rice." Heidi's face showed clear disappointment.

She was missing the point. Paul said, "Yeah, I didn't say we were going to like the food. Only that we'd have something to keep us alive, just in case."

Heidi leaned forward and put her elbows on the table, entirely serious. "You know this sounds a little nuts, right?

I'm not saying you're nuts, but you know, people might think that. Do you really think there's a danger?"

Paul leaned back and tried to look casual. "No, not really. I just worry about it, that's all. I guess I figured a hundred bucks was a small price to pay to assuage my fears over this Ebola thing. We can stick it in the basement and not worry about it. If we need it, it's there. If we don't, we're not going to miss a hundred bucks."

"This isn't like you."

"I know," Paul agreed. "I hate white rice too. But like I said, they didn't have brown."

"No, not the rice. You're always so…I don't know. You don't worry about stuff. That's *my* job, isn't it?"

Paul shrugged. "This one concerns me a bit."

Uncharacteristically wordless, Heidi looked down at her iced tea.

"I'm probably overreacting." It seemed like the right thing to say, and maybe it was. Nonetheless, Paul couldn't shake the feeling that maybe he hadn't done enough. He was trying to find the happy balance between doing enough and feeling embarrassed for doing anything.

Looking back up at him, Heidi asked, "Do you think we'll see an epidemic here, like they're having in West Africa?"

"No." Paul's brow furrowed while he thought about that snap answer. "A lot of people are sick. A *lot*. A lot of people have died. More than in that SARS thing a few years ago."

"It's been going on for three or four months, right?" Heidi asked. "That's a while. So you'd think more people would catch it, right?"

Paul nodded. Her point was valid. "I just don't get how it spread to so many people in that short amount of time.

It's supposedly transferred through bodily fluids, but it seems like too many people are infected for it all to be explained by just that."

"I don't understand. What are you getting at?" Heidi glanced down at her phone. Her newsfeed was calling.

"I'm only speculating, but I wonder if there isn't an airborne strain that's spreading over there."

Heidi shook her head while she thought about it. "Taking the reverse argument, if it *was* airborne and it's been around since March or April, wouldn't a lot more people be infected?"

It was Paul's turn to sit back and ponder. "Yeah. I think you're right. Just the same, we've got some food in the basement."

"You know what worries me?"

"If your phone battery is going to last through the day?" He smiled.

Heidi kicked him under the table. "No. With Austin in Uganda, what happens if the epidemic spreads? Will the university bring him home early?"

Looking at her across the table, Paul saw the worry growing on her face.

"I know he's not my son, but I feel like he is."

Paul grinned. "You're getting maternal?"

Heidi kicked again, but missed. "Don't be a butt. You know how I feel about him."

"Yeah, sorry." Going back to the previous question, Paul said, "I don't know if the university will bring him home early or not. It honestly never crossed my mind."

"Do you want me to call tomorrow and find out?"

Paul knew what that really meant was that Heidi was going to call tomorrow and was just letting him know. Still, things worked better if he played the game. "Yeah, that sounds like a good idea."

"Did he give you any contact information?"

Paul shrugged. "No."

"Didn't you ask?"

"Of course."

"Do you know the name of the program he went there with?" Heidi asked.

Paul shrugged again. "No."

"I thought you asked him for that." There was exasperation in her voice.

"I did ask. I don't remember him emailing me the information."

"Did he send you his contact information in Africa?"

"No." It came out a lot more sheepishly than Paul intended. "I asked him to send it. He just didn't."

"He didn't send you anything? Did you ask again?"

"Don't nag."

Heidi huffed. "You *have* to nag him sometimes. You *know* how he is. This is about his safety in a third-world country halfway around the world. Doesn't it bother you? Aren't you worried?"

"Yeah." One word was all he could get in.

Heidi shook her head. "I swear, Paul. You're lucky you have me around, or you wouldn't know anything about what's happening with Austin. I'll call Texas A&M tomorrow and find out which summer abroad program he went over there with, and I'll find out who his faculty sponsor is, and I'll find out if they have an emergency contingency plan."

"Thanks." Paul tried not to roll his eyes but some things

just happen.

Heidi kicked him under the table again.

Chapter 18

Several dozen five-gallon plastic buckets had been found in one of the farm warehouses, distributed around the ward, and placed between the beds and sleeping mats. The patients weren't allowed to use the outhouses behind the building—new quarantine rules. Not that many of them could have made the walk out behind the hospital anyway. Most couldn't walk to the interior restroom, which ran off the insufficient supply of water in the hospital's cistern. So the door to the interior restroom was ordered locked, leaving the patients with one choice for relieving themselves—the buckets.

Carrying two buckets sloshing with reeking human waste, Austin shouldered his way through a door at the back of the dark ward. The buckets came from beside the beds at the back of the room, from among the first of the patients who had been admitted with high fever, headaches, diarrhea, and vomiting. Most of those also had the rash. Hell, *most* of the patients inside had the rash. It seemed to be spreading across the ward as if it were a disease all its own. Then there were the patients who were bleeding from the eyes, nose, or ears. To Austin, that was the irrevocable sign of hemorrhagic fever—the bleeding.

He crossed the grass behind the hospital and stopped in front of the stinking pit near the tree line. Dumping the buckets, he couldn't help but notice black tarry lumps in the red and brown liquid. Nearly retching, he quickly stepped away.

"Their organs are breaking down."

Startled, Austin turned to look.

Nurse Mary-Margaret, with eyes red from lack of sleep

and crying, had followed him out. She'd obviously seen what came out of the buckets and turned away to look up at the grayish mists floating through the tops of giant trees up Mt. Elgon's slopes. At twelve thousand feet the dense forest gave way to bare rock as the mountain reached to touch the sky.

"Breaking down?" Austin asked.

"I started seeing it earlier today."

"What does it mean?"

"The Ebola virus causes blood to clot," she replied.

Austin sat the buckets down. "I'm confused. I thought it made you bleed?"

"Early on, the blood clots in the veins. Those clots clump together and clog arteries. When that happens, dead spots form because flesh that can't get oxygen from the blood dies. This clotting uses up all of the body's natural coagulants."

Austin couldn't help but look down at the residue in his buckets.

"The body starts to slough off the dead flesh. That's what ends up in the buckets, dead flesh from the esophagus or stomach when it is vomited out. When the lining of the intestines is sloughed off it is—" she hesitated.

Austin glanced at his buckets and looked back at the pit —horrified. "It *is* Ebola, then."

Nurse Mary-Margaret nodded, and her face, with her mask pulled down below her chin, was nothing but sadness. "It still makes no sense."

Austin didn't know if he wanted to ask. "Why?"

Mary-Margaret replied, "You mean, how did so many get sick so fast?"

It was a rhetorical question. Of course, Austin didn't

know that answer. "Maybe when the doctor from the WHO gets here, he can help."

"He's here already. He got here about fifteen minutes ago."

Austin perked up. "I didn't see him."

Nurse Mary-Margaret shook her head. "You've been working so hard in here all day. By the way, how are *you* feeling?"

"Like shit."

Nurse Mary-Margaret laughed. "I'm not one to use that word, but I might. We all feel bad. We need help here—thank you for pitching in. But how's your fever?"

"Stable, I guess." Austin touched the back of his forearm—the part above the glove—to his forehead. "I don't feel any hotter. I think the work helps. I don't know."

"You'll end up sick if you push yourself too hard."

"I'm already sick, will it make a difference?"

Mary-Margaret tried to look hopeful. "I wish I could tell you."

"Then I'll keep going as long as I can." Austin looked back into the ward. "You said the doctor from the WHO is here?"

"We've set up another ward in the school."

"Another ward?" And before Austin could think that it was a stupid thing to say, he said, "We're so crowded in here. We should move some of these patients—"

Mary-Margaret's old face stretched sadder with a slow shake, and that answered the question.

"There's no room in the other ward?" Austin asked as though he hadn't already guessed the answer.

"No."

"My God." Austin shook his head. "How many are sick?"

"Three hundred and eleven, at last count."

"How is that possible?" he asked.

"That's what we're trying to find out."

Austin stepped back so that he could see part of the town around the hospital building. "I wonder how many are sick in their homes, afraid to come for help."

"We have volunteers out now, checking."

"Do you think there could be a lot?" Austin asked, shaking his head without meaning to. The hopelessness of the absent, red eyes in the ward was infecting him.

Mary-Margaret said, "There might be more sick people in their homes than here. This isn't Denver. People here don't trust hospitals like they do in the states."

"Jesus." Austin paused and tried to tamp down the frustration coming out in his tone. "Is everybody in the village going to get it? How many people live in Kapchorwa?"

"Maybe eleven or twelve hundred within a mile of the center of town," she replied.

"So between the hospital, the school, and any who are in their houses and afraid to come out, how many do you think are infected? Half? More?" Austin didn't want to believe it.

Large numbers of dying people spread across a desert refugee camp was an easy thing to depersonalize when seen from the perspective of a couch in an air-conditioned room on the other side of the world. Dying people who could be smelled, who could be touched, whose tears flowed out of empty eyes — close enough to wipe away with your own hand — that kind of dying was real in a way that few people have the misfortune to understand. And all around, people were dying—the ones Austin could see and many more that he couldn't.

He asked, "How is it possible that so many could contract it so fast?"

"We don't know." Mary-Margaret shook her head. She looked defeated. "That's why Dr. Littlefield thought at first it might be typhoid."

Austin looked down at the bucket to make his point. "But now we know that's not true."

Nodding on autopilot, Mary-Margaret softly confirmed, "We know that's not true."

Austin squatted to stretch his legs—in a way—to get closer to the ground, so when he passed out and fell over it would hurt less. "So, somewhere between sixty and ninety percent of all of those people are going to die?"

"Depending on which strain of Ebola this is."

Austin thought about all the people he'd seen on the streets, everyone he'd talked to, and those he'd befriended since coming to Kapchorwa—most of them were going to die. And not just die, but gruesomely waste away as their bodies painfully disintegrated from within. He looked at his gloved hands as though he might see something there— evidence that he was alive, or evidence that he might stay that way. "I don't know."

Mary-Margaret turned to Austin, confused. "What? What don't you know?"

"I think I'm numb." Austin shook his head slowly as he spoke. "I never expected anything like *this*. I feel like I just need to keep moving, you know. I'm afraid to stop."

He thought about when he'd been sitting on the plane at Denver International Airport prior to take off. He'd been excited about coming to Africa. It was the grandest adventure he could imagine. But it wasn't just that. He felt a passion to make a difference in the world. He didn't harbor any illusions about making it better for everyone. Those kinds of thoughts were idealistic silliness. Austin's aspirations were much simpler. He wanted to make the world better for *someone*, or maybe several people. So when he stood in front of his class of a dozen kids in the free school and felt the enthusiasm they had for learning, he knew he was helping them—if only just a little—toward a better life. In some ways, those days were among the best of his life. He was happy. He was making a difference.

But just as life in America has a way of killing the soul with vapid pleasures, life in Africa broke the heart through random brutality. Austin closed his eyes and choked back a tear as he saw a parade of smiling faces of those who lived in the village. Many of those people were in the clinic, and he had been carrying out buckets of their fluids all day. Their eyes were desperate with pain. They knew they were dying. Few of them had any hope.

Ebola was that kind of killer. Through its deadly reputation, it killed hope first. Without hope, victims only wanted the suffering to end. They gave up. And in lingering moments of consciousness, they stared at the ceiling or the dying person in the cot next to them. Some cried. But most were past tears.

Austin couldn't think about it anymore. He needed to get moving. No matter how much he hurt, the work helped. "I'm running out of bleach to clean these."

"We're running out of everything." And that was the end of Mary-Margaret's hope. She put her face in her hands to catch her flowing tears.

Staring at her didn't seem awkward. In weeks past he'd

have turned away, distracted himself with a misplaced comment on something unrelated, random, and maybe even funny. But that's what people he knew back at school did. Back in that sterile, painless world, emotions were hidden—something for keeping behind bedroom doors or in darkened rooms. Emotions were shameful things that were only put on display in books and movies, when fictional characters with imaginary problems had the right to cry, making moviegoers feel their pain so thoroughly that they cried, too.

But painful in America? How bad was that really? Losing a boyfriend? Getting a parking ticket? Missing out on a job? A long line at Starbucks? Getting behind on a credit card payment?

Pain in Africa was getting thrown off of a roof for the sin of being an orphan. It was being castrated in the street and left to bleed out. It was standing in a ward, stinking of death, watching every familiar face lose its smile, lose its hope, bleed its tears, convulse, and die.

Chapter 19

Dr. Littlefield walked across the deserted dirt street, still groggy from his insufficient nap. Wind from a coming thunderstorm kicked up a red dust that blew down the road. Littlefield shielded his eyes as he noticed a truck parked near the hospital entrance. Had help finally arrived?

He mounted the steps and just as he landed a foot on the porch, a tall man in full protective gear opened the door and came out of the hospital. "Dr. Littlefield?" He had a thick Italian accent.

"Yes." Littlefield glanced down at his own inadequate bundle of protective gear—a surgical mask, goggles, gloves, rubber boots, and a plastic apron.

"I'm Dr. Dante Giovanni. I sent the girl to wake you."

"Thank you for coming, Doctor."

"You're an imbecile." Dr. Giovanni sounded like a father who'd lost all his patience with a child who didn't want to learn. "You are going to kill everyone in this town."

Dr. Littlefield's immediate impulse was to lash back, but he didn't have the energy for it. Too many twenty-hour days had worn all the fight out of him.

"I've only been here a half hour, and I can already see this is Ebola—or maybe Marburg—if you're lucky. And what have you done? Your nurses wear plastic aprons they've been reusing for days. They clean the aprons in a common bucket instead of burning them. They are not protected from this outbreak. You're going to kill them *and* yourself. You don't have a containment area. You let people walk out of the hospital and into the street, carrying the virus with them. You've made this whole town a hot zone. How can you be a doctor in this country and not have the good sense to take the proper steps to contain this?"

Dr. Giovanni was on the edge of the porch by then, Littlefield having backed down a few steps in the face of the scolding.

But Giovanni's rebuke found a quick end. "Have you *nothing* to say for yourself?"

"Yes. Are you ready to listen?" Littlefield replied.

"Of course." It sounded like a platitude.

"I'll skip right over the part where I tell you I've been on the radio, and you're the first person to show up." Littlefield retreated down the last few steps and put himself on level ground. The Italian could come down and talk to him face-to-face.

Dr. Giovanni proceeded down the steps and took up a position on the dirt road in front of Littlefield, towering over him anyway. "I came to investigate as fast as I could."

"When were you told to come?" Littlefield was not impressed, and his tone made that very clear.

"Yesterday morning?"

"Why so long?"

"West Africa." That was the simple answer, and both Littlefield and Giovanni knew that. West Africa was experiencing the largest Ebola outbreak in history, and it was accelerating. "Whoever is not there is running around the rest of Africa chasing rumors of more outbreaks. Most of them are just fear."

Littlefield nodded to the hospital. "But this one isn't, is it?"

"No. But if you know it's Ebola, why haven't you taken the steps to contain the disease?"

Dr. Littlefield laughed harshly. "It's so easy to judge, isn't it?"

Dr. Giovanni took a moment to pull himself back from the edge of losing his temper. "Tell me, then. What happened here?"

"As far as containment goes, well, you can see the outbreak is bad. It's already everywhere in the town."

"When did it start?"

Littlefield did some mental math. "People started showing up with symptoms a week ago."

Dr. Giovanni asked, "How many?"

"A lot more than there should have been for a normal outbreak. Nearly two dozen that first day." The fog of missed sleep clouded his memory.

"Twenty-four?"

"Yes." Littlefield looked down, nodding for emphasis. "Twice that number, the next. On the third day, when I started pleading for help, we had around a hundred. That is a lot for a town this size."

"And you're the only doctor?"

Littlefield gestured down the street. "This is not a large town. Even so, maybe a hundred thousand live in the district. There are two other small clinics in the area, but this is the only one that passes for a hospital. There *were* two of us, but Dr. Ruhindi is inside. He fainted last night. He has the virus, and can't even stand now. Two of our nurses went to Sierra Leone two months ago to help. Some of the college students teaching at the free school volunteered to help. All but one is sick. We have Nurse Mary-Margaret and a couple of girls from the town who help us."

"When did you first suspect Ebola?"

Littlefield thought for a moment. "The third day. Before that, patients had the usual headaches, fever, nausea, and diarrhea that accompany just about any common outbreak. However, this outbreak was so widespread and sudden, I initially suspected typhoid. I drew blood samples and sent them to the lab in Kampala."

"What came back?"

"Nothing."

Putting the pieces of the puzzle together, Giovanni replied, "You didn't receive the results?"

"I'm still waiting."

"You may not ever get the results. Rumors of Ebola and fear of the disease have caused the government to blockade the roads in most of the eastern districts."

"Great." Dr. Littlefield stepped over to lean against the side of the porch's foundation, and put himself under the shade of the roof that slanted out in front of it. "On the third day, maybe twenty of the people who'd come in over the previous days with other symptoms came back with blood-red eyes. Others followed. The rashes started showing up, and that's when I knew."

"But all at once? How do you explain it?"

Dr. Littlefield shook his head. "It didn't make any sense. You obviously see that, too. Ebola has a death chain. Usually you can trace it back one person at a time. Perhaps a man comes in with symptoms, but you know he got it from his wife, who was in two weeks ago, who got it from their child, who contracted the disease a week or two before. And maybe that child got it from a childhood friend. Ebola is a nightmare—a slow-motion nightmare that grows through personal contact. It thrives in this culture because they feel a social need to touch. They even touch the bare skin of the dead in their funeral rituals."

"Not that different than us in the West," Dr. Giovanni

said.

"I guess not." Dr. Littlefield took a moment to collect his thoughts and get himself back on track. "We didn't have a death chain here. That's the reason I didn't even suspect Ebola at first."

"Because it exploded across the population rather than growing in it?" Dr. Giovanni asked.

"Yes. That's exactly what happened. It exploded for no apparent reason. People were getting infected by the dozens, with no apparent link. Of course, that was at first. By now, everybody in town who didn't flee is in some stage of the disease. The hospital is overflowing." Dr. Littlefield pointed to a cluster of three rectangular buildings a short distance across the mountain slope. "The school buildings are full."

"Everybody is infected?"

"I don't know that for sure." Dr. Littlefield pointed down the road in both directions. "Two days ago I walked through town and tried to get people to come out of their houses and talk to me."

"And?"

"Most wouldn't come out. The ones who did kept their distance, which was smart. A few admitted that at least someone inside was sick. In some houses, everyone is sick. Everyone. But they were afraid to come to the hospital."

"Do you blame them?" Dr. Giovanni asked.

"No. There's little we can do for them. Most of our protective equipment was stolen early on."

"That's what happened to it?"

Dr. Littlefield nodded sadly. "What you see is what we have."

Dr. Giovanni started to raise his hand to shake, but

quickly put it back down. "I'm sorry. I owe you an apology."

"You do," Littlefield agreed. Giovanni had been unnecessarily harsh.

"I admire your dedication and bravery."

Dr. Littlefield glanced at the hospital doors over his shoulder. "I'm just trying to help."

"Are *you* symptomatic yet?"

"I have a headache and a fever," Dr. Littlefield admitted.

"I'm sorry."

Littlefield shook his head. "It was inevitable." And for so many caregivers in Africa that was indeed the case. He walked around Dr. Giovanni, climbed the six stairs up to the hospital's porch, and went to his favorite spot to lean and look at the small farming community. "I'm afraid."

"Of dying?" Dr. Giovanni asked.

"Something worse."

The Italian doctor waited silently for the explanation.

"Are you familiar with the Ebola Reston strain?"

"Of course. Named for Reston, Virginia. Did I say that correctly?"

Dr. Littlefield shrugged at the accent. "Close enough."

"There was a company there that quarantined monkeys imported for scientific research. I believe they had five hundred monkeys on the premises."

"Yes, that's the place. In the monkey house." Dr. Littlefield's heart sank just to be talking about it—the thoughts had been haunting him for days. "Maybe fifty or a hundred monkeys died before they figured out it wasn't Simian Hemorrhagic Fever, but Ebola. The Army came in and destroyed all the monkeys. I think four people became infected, but didn't die. That strain was damned lethal for monkeys, but it let humans off easy." He stood up straight and looked out across the town.

Dr. Giovanni waited patiently for Dr. Littlefield to finish.

"The monkeys didn't get infected through direct contact. Monkeys in one room had come into the facility with the virus, then monkeys in other rooms became infected and started dying. There was no physical contact between the monkeys."

"What are you saying?" Dr. Giovanni asked.

"Like Ebola Reston—" Dr. Littlefield hesitated. It was a frightening thing to think, a hard thing to say. *"I think this one is airborne."*

Chapter 20

Nurse Mary-Margaret finished crying. Sufficient tears had fallen to let her find her strength again.

Austin was sitting on the ground by then, not caring that the smell was still coming from the buckets or even that it seemed to be permanently burned into his nostrils. He was watching the late afternoon shadows grow across the town.

"Are you okay?" Nurse Mary-Margaret asked.

"I'm okay."

"After you clean those, you should rest," she said.

Austin shook his head and said nothing. He still had a lump in his throat. His thoughts were on Rashid, Margaux, and Benoit. They'd grown close in the previous seven weeks.

He thought about their hike up to Sipi Falls that first time. It was a little bit dangerous, but thrilling and magical. They'd met a coffee farmer up there who'd let them sleep in his storehouse. It was far from fancy—just a dirt-floored shack—but the family's kindness eclipsed the accommodations. To think that a coffee farmer who made less in a year than his dad made in a week was happy to share what he had with some wide-eyed mzungu kids gave Austin optimism for the future of humanity. They'd all become friends after that, and the kids had been up to visit the farmer several times. It was the kind of experience neither he nor his friends would ever dream of back in Denver. It was so much more real than a t-shirt from the Louvre or a postcard from Rome.

Austin looked away from his thoughts and said, "I'll be okay, Mary-Margaret. You go ahead. I'll be inside in a minute."

"Okay." Nurse Mary-Margaret turned and headed back to the hospital.

The familiar sound of tires on gravel caught Austin's attention. On the road coming into town from the east were two Land Rovers, with paint shiny under red dust. Curiosity kept his eyes on the Land Rovers until they came to stop on the road in front of the hospital building. Car doors opened. Men in bright yellow Tyvek suits with hoods, gloves, goggles, and surgical masks got out.

Thank God. The cavalry had arrived.

Chapter 21

The sky was getting dark and the cicadas started their nightly ruckus. Austin walked in through the back door of the ward with clean buckets in hand. Immediately, he sensed something wasn't right.

The guys in the yellow HAZMAT suits nearly glowing in the lantern light had arrayed themselves around the ward, seemingly doing nothing except watching. One was kneeling over Rashid, hands busy. In the center of the ward, three of the Tyvek-clad guys were squared off, facing Dr. Littlefield and Nurse Mary-Margaret in their pitifully inadequate — by comparison — protective gear. Between them stood a tall man in some kind of light blue protective suit.

Austin couldn't make out what was being said, but it sounded tense. The body language was combative.

He quietly crept through the ward, trying not to be noticed, placing the empty buckets back in the spots where they'd been, and carefully navigated around the rows of patients to get to the center aisle, a six-foot wide strip up the center of the building. It was the only part of the floor not covered by a cot or colorful plastic woven mat.

Careful not to get too close to Dr. Littlefield and the others, he worked his way across the rows of villagers lying on the floor. He approached Rashid from the opposite side of the man who was tending to him.

Things weren't making sense. The HAZMAT-covered aid workers weren't rendering aid to anyone except Rashid. Austin looked down at Benoit as he stepped over him. Benoit was unconscious, pale, and splotched. Austin knelt beside Rashid and said to the person in the yellow suit,

"Who *are* you?"

The man in yellow looked up at Austin, said nothing, and went back to his work.

Seeing that one of the men in yellow was coming toward them, Austin said to the man at Rashid's side, "I'm Austin Cooper. This is my friend, Rashid." When the man didn't respond, Austin ventured a guess. "Are you Najid? I'm the one who called you."

The other Tyvek-clad man arrived and roughly put his hand on Austin's shoulder.

The guy at Rashid's side gestured to the other and the hands came off of Austin. He said, "I am a doctor. Mr. Almasi brought me here."

"Najid Almasi? Rashid's brother?" asked Austin.

"The same."

Austin looked down at Rashid. "Can you help him?"

"I don't know."

Austin was finding it very strange talking to a man clad in a yellow Tyvek suit, with goggles and a duckbill-shaped surgical mask. He felt like he was talking to a mannequin. "Is it Ebola?"

"It would seem."

"Do you have a name?" Austin asked.

"Yes."

Austin waited for the name, but the yellow doctor didn't share it.

The doctor pointed at a big cardboard box in the center aisle that had gone unnoticed by Austin until the doctor pointed. The doctor said something in Arabic, and the man with the rough hands knelt down and dug into the box, coming out with a few IV bags. He brought them over and elbowed Austin aside.

Keeping his comments to himself, Austin stepped to the other side of Benoit, becoming aware of raised voices coming from the people at the center of the ward. Looking around, he figured the guys in yellow Tyvek were together. The guy in the blue plastic suit, with goggles and mask, had to be the doctor from the WHO Nurse Mary-Margaret mentioned. He was pissed and raising his voice as he towered over the other men in yellow. The angrier he got, the more pronounced his Italian accent became, until Austin heard a word that took his breath away.

"Airborne."

Airborne?

Oh my God.

Austin had no medical training but he knew enough to understand that the words Ebola and airborne were a bone-chilling combination.

"Ebola is *not* an airborne disease." The man at the center of the yellow trio was doing the talking for the Tyvek-clad group. His stance and the tone of voice indicated he was in charge. Austin surmised he was Najid Almasi.

"Look around, you fool!" the Italian man yelled. "There is no explanation for all of this except Ebola. Even if it isn't airborne, how could you take the chance? Do you know how many people you would kill if it *is* airborne? Do you? Including yourself? Is *that* what you *want*?" The Italian doctor looked past Najid at the other HAZMAT guys, and yelled, "Is that what *any* of you *want*?"

Not a one of them reacted to the outburst.

Dr. Littlefield said, "Please, Mr. Almasi, I'm asking you not to take Rashid out of here. But *do* understand, I *will* forbid it. This is not a decision for the family to make. It is a medical decision."

"You forbid it?" Najid laughed. "You are mistaken, Doctor."

The Italian doctor spoke up, "No, *you* are mistaken." He pointed at Rashid. "That boy will not leave this place until he has recovered. Do you understand?"

Najid didn't say anything after that, instead staring inscrutably from under his protective gear.

The Italian doctor wasn't intimidated. He put his hands on his hips and made it clear that he had no intention of considering any position other than his own.

After a few tense moments, Najid abruptly turned, and without a word walked toward the door. As he passed Rashid's bed, he said something in Arabic to the doctor. The doctor responded with a few Arabic words. Except for the doctor at Rashid's side, all of the other men in bright yellow filed out after Najid.

Austin looked at Dr. Littlefield, the Italian doctor, and Nurse Mary-Margaret. They seemed as surprised as Austin.

A moment later, Rashid's doctor came to a stopping point, stood up, and followed the others out the door.

Chapter 22

It wasn't that Paul Cooper was pro-gun or anti-gun. He simply didn't have one. He didn't have any interest in hunting. He didn't worry that his house would be burglarized or that he'd get mugged and have to shoot the mugger. He never imagined himself taking up arms against the government or threatening to shoot the neighbor's dog. And though he often fantasized about shooting holes in the cars of particularly obnoxious drivers, those thoughts never evolved past the fantasy phase. There was no scenario in Paul's imagination that required him to have a gun in his hands.

However, when the fifth case of Ebola on American soil was reported on the news, he worried. And he worried enough to find himself sitting in his truck before work, parked in a little strip mall parking lot, ambiguously positioned for access to the little barbecue joint or the gun store next door—a gun store he knew about only because it was next door to the barbeque joint—the only gun store he could find without Googling.

Five cases of Ebola in New York in two days.

The first had prompted that trip to Costco. Now he was sitting in front of a gun shop wondering if he was crazy for thinking prepper thoughts. Did Colorado have a mandatory waiting period on handguns? Would he pass a background check? Did that even pass in the last election? What about assault rifles? An AR-15 would be cool. At least that's what he'd been thinking in the back of his mind ever since he'd held his buddy John's AR-15. What about a shotgun? He remembered hearing that shotgun purchases didn't require a waiting period. But the truth was, there wasn't a thing he knew about guns that he didn't pick up from watching TV. That meant he probably knew just enough to hurt himself with a gun.

And that brought his thoughts back around to the top of the circle. Did he need a gun? Was he overreacting to the news?

He'd had similar thoughts when he was stocking up with prepper food at Costco. And though it embarrassed him when Heidi told the neighbor, he felt better knowing he had it. Why? Because if an Ebola epidemic spread across the country, everything would go to shit. Of that, he was sure.

With people bleeding out in the street from Ebola, who would go to work at the grocery store—or anywhere for that matter? When contact with a coworker or a customer could lead to a horrific death, going to work would be the last thing on anyone's mind. Not even the police or the National Guard would be on duty. They'd all be home, either afraid of the virus, or choosing to put the protection of their families above the protection of strangers. Not an unreasonable position to take.

That implied supply systems would break down. Law and order would crumble. Power systems might stop delivery, and water might stop flowing. The most modern country in the world would take a hard backward turn to the Dark Ages, leaving three hundred million people a few days or a few weeks away from their first ever experience with real hunger.

That's when things would turn ugly.

Paul was a parent. And whenever he asked himself that one question—what wouldn't he do for the welfare of his children—the answer was always the same. There was pretty much *nothing* he wouldn't do for his children's sake.

It stood to reason that other parents felt the same.

That led to the next step in the logical chain. A parent who had to look at his starving children would go to the grocery store and get the last of what was available, despite the infection risk and the risk that bad people would be out doing bad things. But it wouldn't be long before even those grocery store shelves emptied out. Where would a man with hungry children turn after that?

The neighbors' houses. That was the simple answer.

He'd look at his neighbors, but he'd be afraid to go into the houses where the residents had died of Ebola. Instead, he'd open his gun safe and decide that his odds were better going to the house of the guy who'd put the Obama sticker on the back of his car while living in one of the reddest counties in the country.

Because in Paul's mind, people who voted Republican were more likely to own a gun than people who voted Democrat. He guessed he wasn't the only person in the country who thought that way. So that bumper sticker — long since removed — was a target for those neighbors of his who remembered he'd put it there. It said, *Come take my food. I don't have a gun.*

Of course, Paul knew he could be wrong. He was letting his fears run around in escalating circles, but he still thought rationally enough to know that. As he sat in his truck, looking at the gun shop, smelling barbecue, and working himself into a panic, he couldn't get past the fear that Ebola was coming. And when the food ran out, his neighbors that were still alive were coming, too. They'd have their guns, and thanks to Heidi, they'd know he had a hoard of food in his basement.

Paul needed a gun.

Chapter 23

Standing on the porch, evaluating his options, Najid waved his men away. "Dr. Kassis, stay up here with me."

The other six men spread out by the Land Rovers and took to keeping lookout over what they could see of the village in the dark.

Najid turned to Dr. Kassis. "Do you think they are lying?"

"Who is to say? I was never good at reading other men's hearts."

"Always loathe to commit." Najid's derisiveness came through. He had respect for the doctor, for his skill and his loyalty, but deep down the man was never brave enough to speak his mind. "What they were saying about the virus being airborne. Does that make sense?"

The doctor looked back at the door they'd just come through. A ward full of dying townsfolk lay beyond. "I have no reason to believe they lied about the rapidity and seeming universal spread of the disease. If I accept that—" he looked back at the small collection of houses and businesses that made up Kapchorwa, and took a deep breath, "—I would have come to the same conclusion."

"Would you be right?"

"Maybe," the doctor replied.

"That is a guess even I could make. Tell me what you think the chances are."

Dr. Kassis looked at the porch and used the toe of his rubber boot to grind something into the concrete while he thought. "Tomorrow's reality—if this *is* an airborne strain of Ebola—is *so* horrific that it begs me to hope the evidence I seem to see here is wrong. But if these were our people, and this outbreak was in our homeland, I would say the same. I would beg for help from the WHO, even the Americans. I would beg you not to take Rashid out of here until I knew the disease was not airborne."

"And how can I find out for sure?" Najid asked.

"That would be a long process with many tests and many specialized doctors, and he could die before we find out. Otherwise, we may not know for months."

"But if it is airborne, that knowledge will come too late for these people, am I right?"

"You are correct." Dr. Kassis nodded obsequiously. It was a habit of Kassis's that irritated Najid endlessly.

The doctor went on to say, "On this continent, it will be obvious to every doctor that this strain of Ebola is airborne a long time before the tests confirm it. It will be obvious in the mountains of bodies—bodies of the millions who die because they have no access to healthcare that could potentially save some of their lives." He was looking out at the dark sky when he absently repeated, "Some."

"What will happen then?"

"As soon as that Italian doctor notifies his superiors and convinces them to come, the world will start to change. Slowly at first, but as the evidence builds over the coming days and weeks, the Western countries will close down every airport in the world. Commerce will stop. They will do whatever they can to save their own people. They will have their telethons, make ads showing sick children, cry for the suffering, but this part of the world will still be ravaged by the disease."

"And the mortality rate?" asked Najid.

"Of this strain—if it is a new strain—mortality can't be known until the bodies are counted. Marburg, the only other Filovirus we know of, kills a quarter of those infected. Ebola Zaire is a vicious strain and kills ninety percent. Other strains kill as few as sixty."

"With medical treatment will the mortality rate drop significantly?" Najid asked.

"Anecdotally, I must say yes, but Ebola, as frightening as it is, is rare. It hasn't been studied enough for us to know the effects of treatment for certain."

Najid eyed the doctor. "So only one in ten might be alive at the end."

Dr. Kassis gestured to the hospital doors behind them. "You see how it is here. A disease that infects so many so fast does not have to do all the work of killing on its own. There are people in there who with good medical care might survive, but the medical staff and the facilities are overwhelmed. They have run out of everything they could use to treat these people. Many of these will die of secondary infections and causes. The death toll may surpass ninety percent wherever the disease attacks third-world populations."

Analytical as always, Najid couldn't help but ask more questions. "That makes sense to me, but is there medical data to back this up?"

Dr. Kassis looked at Najid. "How much do you know of Marburg virus?"

"I read much about these viruses on our trip here. However, I am certain that my knowledge is shallow. Please, tell me what you know."

"Marburg virus was originally discovered in Germany — in Marburg, of course. So even though the virus was completely new to the doctors and the patients involved, of the thirty-one people infected, only seven died, nearly twenty-three percent." Dr. Kassis concluded with half a shrug. "Modern country. Modern facilities."

Najid leaned against the porch railing. "So it is not as lethal as Ebola."

"No." Dr. Kassis leaned on the railing beside Najid. "In Durba, in the late nineties, an outbreak of the familiar strain of Marburg and a new strain killed eighty-three percent." The doctor pointed southeast. "That was in Congo, during a period of upheaval. People had little or no access to medical treatment. Again, in Angola in 2005, during one of the incessant civil wars, Marburg killed ninety percent. The people had no access to medical care. In my opinion, medical care makes all the difference in the survivability of these diseases."

Najid smiled behind his mask, both for the fact that Dr. Kassis took the risk to volunteer an opinion, and for confirmation that he'd done the right thing in bringing the doctor to treat Rashid.

The doctor continued, "Imagine what will happen with Ebola, with its sixty to ninety percent mortality rate, when the number of cases overwhelms the fragile medical systems of the Third World." He gestured at the closed doors. "As is happening here. It frightens me."

"What of this experimental drug, ZMapp?" Najid asked. "I read they are treating infected American doctors with it."

Dr. Kassis nodded. "And they seem to be responding well."

Najid snorted disdainfully. "But there is only enough for a few Westerners, while Africans die by the hundreds. By the thousands tomorrow. Perhaps by the millions soon."

Najid continued to speculate. "And all while the West hides on the other side of the oceans, hoarding their supplies and doctors, frantically working to mass produce their vaccines and treatments. It appears they may even succeed. All while they wring their hands and shed their crocodile tears over dying Africans and dying Arabs."

The doctor nodded.

"At the end of it, months from now, the disease will reach their shores—that is inevitable—but by then they will be prepared. Over here, most of us will already be dead."

"That may be true," Dr. Kassis agreed.

"They will get what they've always wanted."

The doctor took a moment to adjust his mask that felt like it was slipping down his face. "What's that?"

"Africa, the Middle East, probably even China, and more. Everywhere Islam or communism is strong, the people will suffer and die, leaving the world to the West. *That* is what the West has always wanted—unchallenged power to exploit the resources of the world. Those of us who remain will be too weak and too few to do anything about it."

Dr. Kassis adjusted his goggles to cover the top edge of his surgical mask. "Sadly, I can't disagree with your analysis."

"What would you do if you were me, I wonder?" asked Najid.

"I can't—"

"Answer me honestly, Kassis. If only this one time in your life. Tell me what you would do."

Kassis scraped the toe of his rubber boot on the concrete again, grinding into nothingness whatever was there. "I love your brother like my own son. But to bring him back may bring death to everyone you know. If I were you, I would leave Rashid in my hands to treat. I won't tell you that I can save him. I can only tell you what I told you before we came, that I can give him a better chance to live. But you should leave this place. Go home and pray."

When Najid spoke again, Kassis flinched, as though he were expecting harsh treatment for his bad choice to speak the truth. But Najid replied, "We are different men, with different stations in the life, different burdens. Thank you for your honesty, Dr. Kassis. I will ask that from this day forward, you speak your mind openly and honestly whenever I ask. I will not like what you tell me—I assure you I won't. But I will need your honest counsel."

"You shall have it then," replied the doctor.

"Your trepidation will go away in time." Najid put a hand on Dr. Kassis's shoulder. "We came here to save my brother, nothing else. But I see now that Allah has led me here for another purpose."

Najid called to one of his men, commanding him to retrieve the weapons from the SUVs. To the doctor, he said, "If this Ebola is airborne, it will kill many—if not most—men. That is a horror I cannot do anything about. I find it equally horrifying that the West may come through this unscathed. I will not allow that. I will not cede the world to them through my own inaction. Allah put me here for a reason. And that reason is to make this decision. When this disease ravages mankind, it will not be only brown bodies on the funeral pyres and in the mass graves."

Chapter 24

Austin stepped over arms and legs sprawled off the sides of mats and cots as he made his way to the center aisle. When he was in front of the doctors, he asked, "Is it really airborne? Did it mutate?"

The Italian didn't say anything.

Dr. Littlefield said, "Austin, I hope to God we're wrong. But that seems to be the case."

"We can't know for sure without testing," Dr. Giovanni said. "Regardless, transporting that boy is the stupidest thing that can be done for him and for public health." He pointed at the front doors through which Najid and his men exited. "That man is an idiot."

"We need to keep this strain isolated in Kapchorwa," Dr. Littlefield added. "We can't let Rashid leave."

Austin pointed at the door. "What about *those* guys? How are you going to keep *them* here?"

"They'll listen to reason," Dr. Littlefield replied.

The Italian doctor said, "It won't matter. I need to get my phone and make a call. It's in my pocket but I can't take it out, not in here. I need to get this suit off, and—"

"Is it a satellite phone?" Nurse Mary-Margaret asked. "If it is a cell phone you'll have to call when you're on the road back to Mbale. Our network is down."

"It happens all the time here," Dr. Littlefield added.

"It is a satellite phone," Giovanni confirmed.

Dr. Littlefield turned to the Italian doctor, "You should go make that call." He turned to Austin and in a quiet voice said, "Would you go outside and write down identifying information on those trucks they arrived in, just in case they decide to leave? I doubt they'll follow proper decontamination procedures when they take off their gear. They could carry the virus with them when they go."

Austin hurried toward the door. Before he got there, it opened, and he froze. Marching back inside were the men in the yellow Tyvek suits. One held a pistol, one a machete, two had AK-47s. The back door of the ward swung open. Three other yellow-suited men with AK-47s came in that way.

"Shit."

Chapter 25

The HAZMAT guy with the pistol came to a stop a few paces in front of the dumbfounded doctors and started talking. Austin knew it was Najid. It was the same terse tone he'd heard on the phone.

Najid pointed the pistol at the tall Italian doctor. "You have a phone. Tell me where it is."

The Italian took a defiant stance. "Go away little man. This is a hospital."

Najid raised his pistol higher and pointed it at the center of the Italian's face.

Dr. Littlefield raised his hands. "This isn't necess—"

"Quiet," Najid shouted. Everyone who still had enough wits to understand hushed.

Austin, without even thinking, was backing up in small steps, away from the tension, away from the raised weapons.

Najid said to the Italian doctor. "The phone."

"No."

Austin admired him for his bravery.

Najid looked to his right. The HAZMAT man with the machete sprang forward. He raised the blade high and brought it down on Nurse Mary-Margaret, catching her where the neck meets the shoulder. It cut deep, with the sound of a breaking bone, a gasp, and a shriek. Nurse Mary-Margaret crumpled to the floor. A few of the patients screamed.

Austin was struck dumb—paralyzed—as were the two doctors. His eyes were wide with fear. Why would they attack *her?*

The machete man raised the blade back and hacked once again into Mary-Margaret's back. She grunted from the impact and blood poured out of her mouth. The machete man then hacked twice more across the back of her neck, and Nurse Mary-Margaret's head rolled to the side as a bloody fountain spewed into a growing puddle on the floor.

Najid looked at Austin, then back toward the Italian doctor.

Austin looked at the front door and judged his chances of making it through. Just about zero. But he wasn't going to stand by helplessly and end up hacked with a machete.

Najid said, "Doctor, your phone. Where is it?"

The Italian doctor's defiant stance sagged into a slump as he looked down at the bleeding body of Nurse Mary-Margaret.

"The phone."

Seconds ticked by as Austin accepted that they were the last of his life as he prepared to run for the door.

The Italian doctor said, "It is in my pocket."

"Give it to me."

The Italian doctor pulled off his protective mask, pulled back his hood and put his hands on the seam down the front of his blue suit. He pulled the seam apart and dropped the suit down over his shoulder, emerging from his protective cocoon with his defiance reborn, glaring at Najid. He put his hand in his pocket, pulled out his phone, pushed a button, and started dialing a number.

For a moment, Najid did nothing, but when the muted ring sounded through the quiet ward and the Italian raised the phone to his ear, Najid pulled the trigger. A spray of blood exploded from the back of the Italian's head. The phone hit the floor as the doctor fell on his back.

Najid smashed the phone with the heel of his rubber boot, crushing the glass, and rendering it useless.

Najid looked at Dr. Littlefield. "Your phone?"

He pointed to the exam room. "It's in there in the drawer on the right. It's not a satellite phone, and there's no service out here."

Najid motioned to the man with the machete, who turned and walked hastily into the exam room. Najid turned his attention to Austin.

Austin didn't need any instructions. He immediately reached under his apron and into his pocket, sure that he was leaving plenty of virions on his clothes. He was already infected, so what did it matter? He dropped his phone on the floor and stomped on it.

"Good boy," Najid turned away from Austin, said something in Arabic, and motioned toward the patients and the few African nurses. A few of the HAZMAT men went to work checking patients and their bedding for phones, showing no concern for the people themselves—pushing them aside, rolling them over, throwing blood-stained pillows and blankets out of their way. The phones they found were immediately destroyed.

"Why are you calling me?" Zameer asked.

Najid hesitated, looking for the right words. "An emergency."

"What kind of emergency would you need my help with?"

"I need our special friends."

There was a long pause. When Zameer spoke, he used a scolding tone. "You should not be calling me about this. You *know* who listens."

"I know." Najid knew there'd be some posturing and he was prepared to be patient—through some of it.

Zameer snorted. "Yet you call."

"As I said, this is an emergency."

"Tell me what you need so I can end this call before a drone flies over and kills my family." Zameer was not pleased.

"You are not *with* your family," replied Najid.

"You know which family I mean."

"I do." Najid was arriving at the end of his patience. "I need *all* of our special friends."

Zameer forced a laugh. "You're insane."

"I am not."

"It cannot happen, my friend. You know of their importance to *his* plans."

Najid paused before answering. "I do."

"And you ask as though you have the right. You may have a rich father—"

Najid felt a boldness rise in his chest. "A *very* rich father who may not live through the month. A father whose wealth I already control."

"Why do I care about the wants of a rich boy who plays at hating the Americans, but rolls in their money?"

Najid thought about having Zameer killed by one of his contacts in the ISI, Pakistan's intelligence agency. "I will get *his* approval. But I need our special friends on an airplane before the sun sets tomorrow."

"That is impossible." Zameer laughed again. "I told you. This is not for you to decide, but him."

"He will agree." Najid did little to mask his impatience. "I have a man on the way to speak with him now."

"After your man speaks with him, I will be told in the usual way, and if he wants our special friends to go to you, they will. That is the end of it."

Najid pretended to think about his next statement but he knew where the conversation would go before he dialed the number. "I will pay you fifty-thousand US for each."

The offer had the desired effect. Zameer was speechless.

Sensing that he had found the sweet spot, Najid continued, "I will have the cash put in your hand personally to do with as you wish. It can be in your hands as early as tomorrow if you deliver our special friends to the airport in Lahore, dressed in the clothes that you received them in."

"Their Western clothes?" Zameer asked.

"Yes."

Zameer paused, "Even if I wanted—"

"Do not play that game with me. You want the money. Let us not disrespect one another with lies."

"Do you know how much money we're talking about?" Zameer's skepticism was apparent.

And with that question, Najid knew the deal was done.

The rest was a matter of running through the pretense so that Zameer would be able to sleep with a clean conscience. Najid said, "I know *exactly* how much."

"It won't matter," Zameer answered. "He will have me killed before I have a chance to spend any of it."

"I told you. You'll have his permission before our special friends board their planes. I merely pay you now for expediting the process."

"Time is that important?" asked Zameer.

"It is."

"American money?"

"Yes," Najid replied flatly.

Zameer confirmed the only real detail. "To have them in the airport at Lahore, we would have to leave tonight."

"You are being compensated for just such inconveniences," Najid answered.

"I don't know."

Najid had other calls to make. "Yes, you do. Don't haggle with me. Take the money or I'll call someone else who will. I do not threaten, but I must have this done today. You know as well as I that the next person I call may not have your degree of moral certitude. He may shed his morals and put a bullet in your skull to get his hands on that money. You, my friend, will make sure that this is handled as we discussed, with *his* blessing."

Rattled, Zameer said, "I will do it."

"You will need to act quickly to get our special friends down from the mountains and to the airport in Lahore. The first flights leave at noon. Do not be late."

Chapter 27

Christoph Degen sat in the summer sun on the balcony of a room he'd rented for an amount that would seem obscene to the average Swiss man or woman. Those thoughts bothered him from time to time, but Zermatt—one of the most beautiful little mountain towns in the world—filled the valley below the hotel. Green mountains rose to the right and left and framed the Matterhorn in picturesque perfection down past the other end of the valley.

From where he sat he could see part way down the main road through Zermatt. He'd watched his wife and two daughters stroll the street, gawking in windows as they started their day of shopping. They were happy. He was happy. Summer holidays in Zermatt were magical.

And then the phone rang. Degen took the phone from his pocket as it rang the second time, saw who it was, and his vacation time—for the moment—became irrelevant. "Good afternoon, Mr. Almasi."

"Mr. Degen," Najid Almasi answered.

"What can I do for you today?"

"What is the value of my father's portfolio?"

"It will take me a moment to pull up that information on my computer." Degen walked back into his room and sat at his desk. His laptop sat open where he'd left it. In a condescending tone, Degen added, "You *are* aware that you can access this information from your computer."

"As can you." Najid was used to the way many Europeans still talked to Arabs, as if they weren't educated at the same schools. "Tell me the number when you have it."

Najid heard the sound of fingers on a keyboard, a pause,

and then Degen's voice. "Seven hundred and thirty-seven million in US dollars. Do you need the exact amount?

"I need you to liquidate the portfolio."

"Mr. Almasi. I don't think—"

"Stop." Najid said it harshly enough to cow Degen immediately. "Before you go on, you *are* aware that I have complete control of my father's portfolio?"

"Yes."

"You *are* aware that I may do whatever I see fit with this portfolio?" Najid could be very abrupt when he wanted something—when he needed something.

"You are the client, Mr. Almasi. Whatever you wish. However, as your financial advisor, it *is* my duty to advise you in these matters."

Najid's patience was already worn thin by previous conversations. "In this matter I do not need advice. I need expeditious action to follow my instructions."

"You do understand that liquidating your portfolio will result in losses on some of your investments. If you'd allow me some time—"

Najid was tiring of the interaction. Degen's was one of a dozen calls he had to make. "I do not have time today to convince you to do what I ask you to do. Will you do it, and do it now?"

Degen didn't answer immediately. He was evaluating his options, or so Najid figured. Either Degen would do as Najid wished, or his superior at the bank would. "I can liquidate most of it. Some of your father's portfolio is traded in foreign markets and cannot be liquidated until those markets open."

"I understand."

"Shall I leave the proceeds in your account or transfer

them to another bank? You understand that for transfer, it is not necessary to sell."

"That is not my purpose. How much of the portfolio can you convert to gold and silver?" Najid had already thought the problem through and had a plan to financially position his family well for the expected outcome.

"Gold stocks are on the upswing, with the Ebola epidemic in Africa driving—"

"You misunderstand, Mr. Degen. Listen carefully. Convert the entire portfolio to cash. Retain thirty million in cash in the account, as I will be drawing on that amount in large transactions. I'll expect that those transactions will come through you personally, and you will see that they are paid as quickly as possible."

"And the rest?"

"Convert it to physical gold and silver—I want at least seventy percent in gold. The gold and silver are to be delivered to my father's compound by noon, three days from now. Earlier if possible. Precious metals that cannot be in my father's compound by that deadline, do not purchase."

Degen gasped. "I understand that you fear the Ebola outbreak, Mr. Almasi, but this step is not necessary."

Najid thought about scolding the man, but chose another tack. "My father is an old man. He doesn't understand the modern world. This is his wish. Like you, I carry out his instructions without question. *Without question.*"

"But the losses—the expense of physically transferring all of that gold?"

"Pay what is necessary to get the gold to my father's compound before noon, three days from now."

"It will be expensive."

"I understand. You will also raise a hundred million in cash, or as much as you can by selling in-the-money call options. I want American-style options that expire in ninety days."

The breath flowed out of Degen in an audible rush.

"You will make commission on this?"

"Yes, Mr. Almasi," replied Degen uncomfortably.

"You will make an enormous sum, will you not?"

"I will."

Najid said, "Then smile when you look in the mirror, as you profit from the ignorance of a man with too much money."

Degen wondered which ignorant man Najid was talking about, himself or his father? "Mr. Almasi, may I speak for a moment?"

"Quickly."

Degen took a moment and proceeded in a calm, measured voice. "Despite the epidemic, the market has been bullish all year. Selling these call options means that as the prices of the underlying securities rise over the next three months, your losses will mount. The analysts at our firm assured me on a conference call just this morning that the trend will remain positive. With the losses you'll take in converting the accounts into physical gold and silver bullion, and the potential losses that you'll incur in a rising market, your father's total portfolio could sink to a fraction of its current value."

"Mr. Degen, thank you for your counsel. One thing we must both keep in mind as we carry out my father's wishes is that this is *his* fortune. You do not have a fortune. You have not earned one. Neither have I. My father did, through shrewd choices. Perhaps it is you and I who are being foolish by questioning his judgment."

"My apologies, Mr. Almasi."

"I'll leave it to you to select the specific financial instruments you sell. Your goals are to raise as much cash as possible and to convert that cash to gold and silver bullion that you will deliver to the appointed place by the appointed deadline."

"As you wish."

"I will call periodically for updates." Najid hung up the phone.

In the next call, Najid bribed the right people to get two shiploads of food aid bound for East Africa redirected the relatively short distance to his father's compound on the eastern shore of the Red Sea. Arms dealers were next on the list.

Chapter 28

One woman in the back of the ward had been bleeding so severely through her nose for the last few hours that she no longer had the strength to hold the towel to her face.

Dr. Littlefield stood beside Austin in the center aisle watching. The woman in the next bed over had been groaning softly with what was presumably the last of her energy. She started to spasm, vomited black, and the bed around her pelvis turned red with her blood.

Dr. Littlefield didn't move. But in a soft, clinical voice said to Austin, "The lining of her stomach died. Her body sloughed it off. That's something you don't normally see except in corpses that have been dead for a few days. That's why it's black." Dr. Littlefield looked at Austin and his eyes were as hopeless as the people dying in row upon row of mats and beds. "Most of these people will die just like that, and there's nothing we can do—not one goddamned thing."

Austin looked around. Faces were slack as though people wore emotionless masks of themselves. When they weren't vomiting and defecating clotted blood into their buckets and beds, they were bleeding out of their gums, ears, noses, and every other orifice. They stared at nothing —dolls or corpses with raspy breaths. Some cried. Most didn't have the energy for that.

When the dying started, Dr. Littlefield had to press their captors to allow the bodies to be removed from the ward. After that, he and Austin were charged with the task of carrying them outside and stacking them beside the pit where Austin had been dumping waste buckets.

Najid's men, still in their yellow Tyvek suits, kept their

distance. A few held their places inside, a few in front of the hospital, a few out behind the building—all with weapons they apparently didn't have any qualms about using.

Chapter 29

The thing that struck Salim the oddest—as he sat in a contoured plastic airport chair, looking across an expanse of shiny terrazzo flooring in the Allama Iqbal International Airport in Lahore—was how much it looked like any airport in America. Only the clothes were different. Of course, some people wore Western clothes. Many wore what looked to Salim like pajamas.

Jalal sat in the chair beside Salim, looking out the tall windows at the airplanes, probably speculating about where they were going, what they'd be doing.

A hundred yards away, Salim was watching Zameer. Probably not his real name, but that's how everyone referred to him in whispers. He didn't know the man's title or position and never asked. Those weren't the kinds of questions to ask when one wanted to keep his head—literally. Salim did know—or suspect strongly—that the guy was in charge.

Salim had seen this man before. He had been through their small camp on three separate visits. Each time, the trainers were nervous and deferential. On one occasion, Zameer berated the trainers loudly, and with more than one slap and a kick to get his point across.

But now, Zameer—short-tempered as he was—stood nervously, shuffling his feet, checking the clock, looking around.

"Where do you think we're going?" Jalal asked in a soft voice that was easily lost in the noise of the airport.

"Far away," replied Salim.

Jalal looked at Salim, disappointment on his face. "We're at an airport. We're in the clothes we wore when we arrived. We have our passports. C'mon Salim, I don't think that guess took a lot of effort."

Salim scanned the terminal again. He was good with faces, and he knew he saw at least two others who had been in the van the day they all arrived in Lahore. Now they were all being sent somewhere internationally. The passports, returned to them with the rest of their possessions, assured that. "We'll know when they give us our tickets."

"We've been waiting for three hours." Jalal's impatience was starting to show.

"Does it matter how long we've been waiting?"

Jalal stood up. "I'm going to the loo." Occasionally, his English dialect seemed out of place.

"I'll be right here when you get back." But as Jalal started to walk away, Salim reached up and caught his sleeve.

Jalal stopped and looked down at him, a question on his face.

Salim asked, "Have you seen any of the others here? I think I've seen a few."

"Who?" Jalal asked.

"Some from the van, the day I arrived."

Jalal looked around. "Good. We're off to do something, I reckon." Jalal spun and hurried off.

Salim went back to watching the formerly important Zameer wait on somebody more important. Salim started to wonder whether he'd see one of the familiar faces from the newscasts back in America—one of those high-profile terrorist targets. Now, *there* was a temptation. What if he did see such a man, with a two million dollar price tag on his head? Was his faith in jihad strong enough not to find a telephone and call in a tip? Was his hatred of America strong enough to keep him from doing it?

Being honest with himself, he didn't know.

Two million dollars would put Salim in a different world. He wouldn't be a powerless middle-class nobody anymore. Perhaps the world looked different when *you* were the one standing on the backs of the poor, rather than being stood upon. And that's how Salim felt—stood upon, powerless, another of the faceless billions under the boot of America's greed.

But to have America's greed working *for* him as he sat on a beach, luxuriating in the dividends that two million dollars' worth of that greed could provide—that might feel pretty good.

The powerful man shuffled some more, walked in a circle, checked his watch, and checked the clock on the wall again.

Jalal sighed as he walked up. "It'll be good to go back to London." He stretched. "I miss the fog."

"You're kidding, right?" Salim shook his head to emphasize his remark. "Fog?"

"No. I'm not kidding. I might be the only Englishman who likes it. I don't know why. But I do."

Salim asked, "How long did you live in London?"

"All my life."

"And your parents?"

"From here. Both from Lahore," answered Jalal.

"How come we never talked about this before?" Salim asked.

Jalal shrugged. "How come you never asked?"

"Such questions are discouraged," Salim answered sadly.

"I know." Jalal grinned. "When your CIA is waterboarding you, you can't tell them what you don't know."

"Seems pointless now." Salim looked for the important man. He seemed to have disappeared.

"How's that?"

"Now that we're off to go somewhere and actually do something. For all we know, we'll be dead tomorrow."

Jalal dropped back into the seat beside Salim, and exhaled a long, slow breath. The gravity of their choices had stopped being a romantic adventure. Youthful self-righteousness was turning into something with real consequences. Jokes about torture at the hands of the CIA might soon stop being funny.

Still unable to see the important man—unable to contain his curiosity, and definitely wanting to keep his options open on that two million dollars—Salim reached out, stretched his arms, and stood up in an attempt to get a better view down to the other end of the terminal.

Where did Zameer go?

Damn.

Zameer had vanished, probably off somewhere with his contact.

Salim thought about walking down to the other end and looking around. That was a gamble. He didn't know if Zameer was meeting anyone of consequence. He did know that to walk away from where they'd been told to wait was a punishable offense. He shuddered to think what that punishment might be.

So he sat down and peered through the sparse crowd, searching the faces he could see.

A man walked up—young, like both of them. "Salim?

Jalal?" he asked.

Jalal looked at Salim with the same question that was on Salim's mind. Yes or no?

Before Salim had chosen how to answer the question, Jalal looked back at the standing man and said, "Yes."

The man extended an envelope to Jalal, turned, and walked off.

"Instructions?" Jalal asked, looking at Salim.

Salim shrugged.

Jalal opened the envelope, reached in and pulled out two tickets. After taking a moment to look at them, he announced, "We're going to Nairobi."

"Nairobi?"

"Our flight leaves in fifty minutes."

Chapter 30

The layover in Dubai was long enough to distract Salim from staring at the back of the seat in front of him, but barely long enough for anyone to get off the plane, except for a few women in black burqas and their chaperones.

Before long, the big jet was back in the air, carrying Salim, Jalal, and possibly others like them, southwest toward Nairobi. Where they were going after Nairobi was a mystery. They had cryptic instructions about taking a cab to some address and waiting on a street corner until they received further instructions.

Salim didn't think they would arrive at the street corner until two or three a.m. And there they'd be, foreigners standing on a corner, in a country neither of them had ever been to, in the middle of the night. If the local police took an interest, how would they explain their presence? They couldn't. Lying would be their only option and lying was pointless. They didn't know enough about anything in Nairobi to construct any kind of plausible lie. They might as well say they'd been abducted by aliens.

Salim was depressed.

He knew it was a matter of faith and discipline — getting on the plane, not knowing where he'd end up, let alone what he'd be doing. Of course, he assumed some jihadist activity awaited him, although at the same time, he felt just as powerless as he always had in America. An outsider. Untrusted. A grunt.

And he started to think that everything had been a mistake. He had the heretical thought that he might not be fighting America to change the world, but fighting simply to put a new repressive authority in power, just one with a different name and different set of corrupt values.

Salim asked Jalal, "Did you like living in London? I mean, besides the fog."

Jalal gave the question some real thought before answering. "Mostly. Did you like Denver?"

Salim nodded. "I think when you can see past the lie that everyone is equal, then yeah, it wasn't so bad. Better than living in the mountains and sleeping in a tick farm."

Chapter 31

Jalal had run out of energy, while walking what seemed like miles across the airport in Nairobi, and he had all but stopped talking. Salim found a cab driver that spoke English. But finding one that spoke English *and* would take them to the street corner where they needed to go—apparently in a less-than-desirable part of town—was another trick.

Nevertheless, by four a.m. they'd been standing on the corner for nearly an hour. Well...Salim stood. After fifteen minutes of waiting, Jalal sat down, leaned against a wall, and dozed off.

Salim wondered if Jalal had doubts about his choice to go to Pakistan and become a jihadist. He realized that the closer they got to wherever they were going, the less certain he was of his course. But here he was in Bumfuck, Africa, with a passport, a backpack, some clothes, toiletries, and enough traveling money to maybe get a meal and a cab back to the airport.

What then? A call to his dad, who suspected—but didn't know—his intentions when he'd disappeared to go to Pakistan? The old man had been furious and broken-hearted. His mother cried. And what was he going to do, get a ride back to the airport? Beg his dad to fly him home? With what? His parents lived paycheck to paycheck to support an outwardly upper-middle class life. They had no savings and a ton of credit card debt. They bought wholeheartedly into the new and improved American Dream—permanent debt that ended in a reverse mortgage, so you couldn't even leave your children the one asset you thought you owned.

Even if Salim could somehow find a way to talk himself

into calling his dad—*if* he could convince his dad to forgive him for his disobedience—there was no way his father could come up with the thousands of dollars on short notice to pay for an expensive last-minute flight back to the US.

Could he find a way? Sure. If he had enough time while waiting around the Nairobi airport. Then again, Salim had seen too many videos of beheadings to think that he would live that long, once it had been found out that he turned against his new brothers.

They would think the only logical things. He was a coward, so he deserved death. He was a traitor, so he deserved death. He was a spy, so he deserved death. He was an apostate, so he deserved death. He was just like every other American, so he deserved death.

He'd never be able to talk his way out of those.

What about the American embassy?

What would he tell them? The truth? He'd gone to fight the Great Satan with his Arab brothers, but had changed his mind. Sure, they'd take him in, listen to all he had to say, probably catch Jalal as a result, and maybe even waterboard them both for a few months before dropping them in Guantanamo to be forgotten forever. Then, when budget and PR burdens became too heavy, some future administration would free him to Yemen or some such place, where he'd promptly lose his head in a desert, all recorded for distribution on YouTube, so that his parents could see their misguided traitor son be murdered by people he was stupid enough to trust.

But he had his passport. There had to be a reason for that.

They'd flown him to Nairobi. There had to be a reason for that.

Perhaps it was the beginning of a plan to ship him back to the US to do his jihad business there. If he was patient, in a few days or maybe even weeks, he'd be touching down in an American city with a network contact, maybe not unlike the one he was waiting on in the middle of the night in Nairobi—*where the hell is Nairobi?* Salim chastised himself for not being a better student in school. He'd be picked up on some anonymous street corner, taken to a safe house. Maybe even told to go out among the Americans and fit in. That would be his chance. He'd find himself a high-priced American attorney to protect his rights, his freedom, and his neck, and he'd trade his information to the FBI or CIA, whichever was in charge of buying it. In return, he'd get immunity and a new identity.

Heck, if he played his cards right, he might even be able to sell the movie rights to his story for a nice bundle of money. Maybe an alternative to the two million dollars he missed out on earlier.

Salim looked up and down the deserted street and didn't care if he got the money. He just wanted to live through the ordeal, as hopes that he'd live to see his next birthday seeped into the darkness around him.

When a van painted in gaudy colors pulled up next to the curb, with friendly lions, zebras, and elephants surrounding the words "Big Country Safari Photo Tours," Salim's hope rekindled. A safari in Nairobi would be a good first step in building a tourism backstory prior to returning to America.

Hope was back in Salim's future.

Chapter 32

"Dr. Wheeler, may I come in?"

Dr. Wheeler looked up from his laptop.

Olivia walked into the conference room. "I was on my way to the cafeteria, and I saw you in here."

"I should have closed the door." Dr. Wheeler smiled widely enough to let her know he was joking. "CDC doctors have lots of groupies."

"I'm Olivia Cooper." She pointed in some direction she doubted meant anything to Dr. Wheeler. "I was in the seminar, in the small theater?"

Wheeler nodded. "I remember you."

"Really?"

"No." He smiled again. "There were a hundred people in there. But I can go on pretending, if you'd like."

Olivia scooted a chair back and sat on the opposite side of the table. "Are you *flirting* with me?"

"I am, if you're open to it, and won't tell my wife."

"You're flirting with me, and you have a wife."

"No, I'm divorced. But we both know I'm old enough to be your dad, and I don't have a chance at getting anything out of this besides a sexual harassment complaint." Dr. Wheeler made an expansive gesture at the building surrounding them. "I assume you work for the NSA."

Olivia looked around the room and gestured at the walls. "This *is* their building."

"Cagey." Dr. Wheeler smiled again. It seemed to come very easy to him. "Okay, I assume you have questions about the Filovirus presentation. Since you appear to have made yourself comfortable, maybe you have a lot of them.

What can I help you with?"

"I'm sorry." Olivia started to stand. "If you don't have time, I can —"

After motioning for Olivia to keep her seat, Dr. Wheeler pointed at his computer, "I'm just answering email. I rode out here from Atlanta with a coworker. He's still in his meeting. I've got some time."

Olivia lowered her weight back down on the chair and smiled. "I'm worried about my brother."

Wheeler leaned back in his chair and looked over his reading glasses. "Because I have a genius-level IQ and I just gave a talk about Filoviruses, is it safe to assume that despite your blue eyes and blonde hair, your brother is an African bushman in Sierra Leone?"

Olivia laughed. "You know I'm only laughing so you'll answer my questions, right?"

"Whatever you need to tell yourself." Dr. Wheeler got comfortable in his seat. "I should warn you, though, my charms are universally appealing. If you feel yourself being mesmerized by the most intelligent — and, I don't mind adding handsome — black man you've ever met, just let me know, and I'll dial it back a bit."

"Are you always like this?"

Dr. Wheeler shrugged. "Yeah. At least my ex said so when she was telling the divorce judge about it." He leaned his elbows on the table. "Seriously, though, you didn't come in here for my comedy routine. What's this business about your brother, and why would I know anything about it?"

"You're an expert in infectious diseases, especially Ebola, which is a Filovirus —"

Grinning, Wheeler said, "So you *were* awake through the first five minutes, anyway."

"—and he's in Africa."

"You're concerned about Ebola." Wheeler nodded, but sounded disappointed, which shifted to boredom when he asked, "Where?"

"Don't do that, please." Olivia thought about getting up to leave.

"Sorry. I've been fielding questions for a month by people who are just sure this Ebola epidemic is going to wipe out the planet. It's all over the news. It's a scary disease, and when people hear about ninety-percent mortality rates with bleeding out of the eyeballs and other less pleasant places, they freak out. You're not freaked out, are you?"

"Sorry." Olivia twirled a curl of her blond hair. "You'd think people would have evolved enough by now to know that hair color doesn't correlate with intelligence. I get overly sensitive when people start talking down to me."

"I apologize. It won't happen again."

"Thanks." Olivia smiled and twirled her hair again without thinking about it. "I know he's probably as safe there as we are here."

"I wouldn't go that far, but I agree with the sentiment."

"He's just not—" Olivia looked for the right word.

"Responsible?"

She shook her head. "No, he's a responsible kid."

"A kid?"

"He's nine years younger than me."

"He's nine?" Wheeler flashed a smile.

Olivia laughed out loud and tried to make it sound mocking. "Does it work when you tell twenty-nine year old girls they look eighteen?"

"It has."

"Really?" Olivia feigned disbelief.

"That whole business I mentioned with the divorce. It started that way."

"You told a girl she looked eighteen, and your wife didn't like it?"

"Oh, you're sharper than I thought. But no, that wasn't it. I married her. We divorced later on. So you're twenty-nine. I guessed wrong. I may not be quite old enough to be your dad. You're not the type to file a complaint with HR are you?"

"Oh, that makes me feel *so* much better."

"It should."

"So your nine-year-old, um, I mean, twenty-year-old brother is in Africa and he's responsible?"

"Yes, but—" Olivia thought about it for a moment. "He's one of those suburban kids who doesn't understand anything about the real world."

"Naïve?"

"Yes, that's a good word."

"So, besides being naïve in a third-world country—which, I might add, could be a good way for him to grow past his naiveté—what has you worried?"

Olivia put on a fake expression of exasperation. "There was the Ebola we talked about."

"Oh, yeah. I think you mentioned that."

She said, "I'm afraid he's not going to take the necessary precautions."

"I'm assuming you're not talking about condoms."

"Dr. Wheeler!"

"You should call me Mathew."

"I think I'll stick with Dr. Wheeler for now." Privately, Olivia was starting to think that maybe she and Mathew could be on a first name basis—except for the age difference, which seemed pretty stark to her. "Let's not talk about my little brother and condoms, okay?"

"You do know that twenty-year-old college boys seldom think about anything that doesn't involve a condom, right? Oh, he is in college, isn't he?"

"Yes, Texas A&M."

"Oh?"

Olivia shook her head. "Dad was a die-hard Texas Longhorn. I think he went there just to piss off my dad."

They looked at each other, idling in their conversational cul-de-sac.

Dr. Wheeler sat up straight and slapped a hand on the table. "Back to business. I'm sure you don't have all day to sit here and flirt with me. Ebola and your brother. What about it? He's not in Liberia, Guinea, or Sierra Leone, is he?"

"Uganda."

"What's he doing there?" Dr. Wheeler asked.

"He's a teacher at a school for street kids."

"Street kids. You mean like the Backstreet Boys?" Wheeler smiled at his humor.

Olivia just shook her head.

"I didn't think it was a bad joke." Dr. Wheeler drew a breath full of mock exasperation. "So, orphans?"

"Yes," answered Olivia.

"That's good. He's in Uganda teaching orphans. He's not a medical worker or anything like that?"

"No." Olivia frowned. "Not even close."

"He doesn't eat undercooked bush meat, does he?"

"Bush meat?" Olivia grimaced. Whatever that was, it didn't sound good.

"Bats, apes, and such."

"Eew."

"Sounds like a no. You probably don't have anything to worry about." Dr. Wheeler's confidence was about as infectious as the disease.

"I know."

"But here you are. And asking questions for a reason."

Olivia looked away. "Yes."

"Do you know how many people died last year of malaria?"

She rolled her eyes and ventured a guess. "Eleven?"

Dr. Wheeler laughed. "Dishing it back out. Okay." He put on a serious face. "Over six hundred thousand. How many died of the Ebola virus last year?"

"None," Olivia answered right away.

"So you've done *some* homework. How about the year before that?"

"Fifty-one."

"How many in the history of the disease? If you don't get this one right, I'll know you weren't listening during my presentation."

Olivia said, "I was so taken with your charm that I didn't catch a single word."

"When you use that much sarcasm, it actually hurts my feelings."

"I'm guessing it just bounces off a deeper layer of ego." Olivia smiled. "Maybe sixteen hundred died of Ebola. The point I guess you're making is that Austin's chances of dying of another infectious disease like malaria are higher than they are of dying from Ebola."

"Astronomically higher," Dr. Wheeler said. "A person can get malaria from a mosquito bite just for going fishing in the wrong spot. You almost have to go out of your way to get Ebola."

"But thirteen hundred cases have been reported in West Africa, and not only is the number increasing, but the curves are becoming steeper. If you graph the number of cases over time, the curve appears to be exponential."

"You *have* done your homework. And you apparently paid attention during your Algebra classes." Dr. Wheeler smiled slyly. "Tell me, why do think that is?"

"Because I liked to be prepared."

"No, I mean, why is Ebola spreading rapidly?" he asked.

"Poor hygiene. Limited availability of medical facilities —"

Dr. Wheeler cut in, "And little trust of the medical infrastructure that exists."

"—cultural norms," she continued.

"Like eating undercooked bush meat. You know certain species of bats are Ebola reservoirs, right?"

Olivia nodded.

"Of course," Dr. Wheeler went on. "You know if people expose themselves to infected flesh, they risk infection themselves. And people there don't have the same cultural inhibitions against eating bats, monkeys, rodents, or anything else they can toss over the fire. Africa isn't anything like Atlanta. We can run down to the grocery store when we get hungry. For most Africans, it's not that simple. You eat what you can get."

"I know that." Olivia didn't need a lesson on the

different levels of affluence around the world.

"Sorry. I'm just making my point."

"Which is?" Olivia asked.

"Ebola is transferred through bodily fluids. That's it."

"There was that test with the pigs and monkeys," Olivia countered.

"Yes, but pigs give off more aerosolized particles than pretty much any other species." Dr. Wheeler pantomimed a gesture to emphasize the point. "A repeat of that study with macaques failed at getting a primate-to-primate transmission. Infected monkeys on one side of the room, clean monkeys on the other. Same setup as with the pigs. The infected monkeys died. The clean monkeys stayed clean and went on to live happy little monkey lives."

"Happy monkey lives as *test animals*?"

"You never know, maybe they're testing the addictive effects of long-term Viagra use right now."

Olivia giggled. Wheeler laughed.

Olivia looked over her shoulder at the open conference room door, feeling slightly self conscious but not sure why. "But the Ebola virus could mutate."

"Are you *trying* to get worked up about this?"

Olivia chose not to answer the question.

Dr. Wheeler leaned forward again, put his elbows on his desk, and scrutinized Olivia for a moment. "Yes. The virus *could* mutate. And before you ask, yes, viruses mutate all the time. I suspect not always for the better—better for the virus, I mean. You know mutation is a random process, although it seems like it's not. Natural selection is *not* random. Once a mutation occurs, nature decides whether it is better or worse for the organism. The vast majority of the time, it's not. The odds of this Ebola outbreak mutating to become more contagious are astronomically small. Don't worry so much."

"Sorry, Dr. Wheeler."

"Your brother will probably be fine. As long as he follows some basic guidelines, he'll come back from Africa healthy. If he comes back with a disease of some sort, the odds are it'll be something other than Ebola."

"What's this about Ebola?"

Both Olivia and Dr. Wheeler looked toward the voice coming from the open door.

Chapter 33

Dr. Wheeler waved Dr. Gonzalez in to join them. "Olivia, this is Dr. Gonzalez, one of my coworkers at the CDC. Dr. Gonzalez, this is Olivia Cooper. She was at my presentation and acknowledges that this is an NSA building, without admitting that she works here."

Olivia spun in her chair to face Gonzalez and extended a hand. "Pleased to meet you."

Dr. Gonzalez pulled away from Olivia.

Dr. Wheeler said, "He's a germophobe."

"Careful is a better word," said Dr. Gonzalez.

Wheeler said, "Olivia and I were talking about her brother. He's in Uganda this summer. I was telling her that he's probably safe from the Ebola outbreak. As you know the outbreak is in West Africa. Uganda is pretty far from there."

Dr. Gonzalez seated himself on the same side of the table as Olivia, but left an empty chair between them, fussily arranging his computer bag on the conference table. "Uganda. Where?"

"Um," Olivia thought about it for a minute. "A little farming town. It's...uh...Kapchorwa?"

"Never heard of it," said Gonzalez. "Wheeler, open up a map of Africa on your computer."

Wheeler rolled his eyes and winked at Olivia.

"I saw that," Gonzalez said. "I'm eccentric, not oblivious."

"Right." Wheeler manipulated the mouse and typed. A few seconds later, he turned the computer sideways on the conference table so that everyone could see the screen.

Olivia leaned forward.

Gonzalez leaned back.

"Zoom in over here." Olivia pointed.

Wheeler did as instructed and zoomed the map in on the eastern half of the country.

Olivia leaned in a little further and pointed to a spot just above a big blob of green. "That's it there, just north of that park." She sat back.

Gonzalez leaned forward. "Zoom out, Wheeler."

Dr. Wheeler fiddled with the wheel on his mouse. "That's Mt. Elgon National Park."

Dr. Gonzalez sighed.

Olivia looked at Dr. Gonzalez, who said nothing to elaborate. She looked at Wheeler. He was wearing his poker face. Olivia frowned and looked back at Gonzalez. "What?"

The doctor opened his mouth to speak as Dr. Wheeler cut him off. "Olivia, before you listen to him, you need to know a quarter million people—maybe more—live within a dozen miles of the base of that mountain."

She looked at Gonzalez. "What? You sighed dramatically like Austin's in Godzilla's backyard."

Dr. Gonzalez pulled a face. "I thought Austin was in Texas."

With a dramatic eye roll, Olivia said, "My brother's name is Austin, Austin Cooper. Now tell me what's wrong? Why the sigh?"

Dr. Gonzalez seemed to think about Olivia's request for a moment as his face went through changes of expression. "You've heard of the Marburg virus?"

"Yes," she answered, using information she'd gleaned from Dr. Wheeler's presentation. "It's similar to Ebola. The first Filovirus discovered. Named for Marburg, the city in

Germany where factory workers at a company making polio vaccines got sick, I think. Thirty-something infected? Seven or eight died?"

"Good memory," Dr. Gonzalez was impressed. "Not to put too much of a scare into you, but the monkeys that carried the virus to Marburg were imported from Uganda."

"That's enough, Steve."

Olivia shot Dr. Wheeler a disapproving look, then shifted attention back to Dr. Gonzalez. "No, it's not. So, the monkeys came from Uganda? That's not necessarily insignificant. Tell me what else."

"In 1980 and again in 1987, Mt. Elgon was connected to outbreaks of the Marburg virus."

"I didn't know that," Olivia replied. "How many died?"

Dr. Gonzalez continued, "Only one in each case. It's not clear how either patient was infected, but both spent time on Mt. Elgon prior to turning symptomatic."

"So there might be a species there that carries the virus, but isn't affected by it." Olivia looked at Dr. Wheeler. "What did you call it? Something of a Typhoid Mary species…a reservoir species."

Dr. Gonzalez paused. "What do you do here, again?"

"Analysis," Olivia answered.

Dr. Gonzalez looked at Dr. Wheeler. "You *must* give a riveting Filovirus presentation."

Dr. Wheeler said, "She's a worrier, but she's a smart one."

Olivia shot Dr. Wheeler a harsh glare with a little smile.

"Is your brother the adventurous type?" Dr. Gonzalez asked. "Is he likely to climb the mountain and go spelunking?"

Olivia's face lost its color. She fumbled around in her

purse for a moment then remembered she left her cell phone in her car. Cell phones weren't allowed inside the building. She looked up at Dr. Wheeler and then at Dr. Gonzalez. "He sent me some pictures a few weeks ago of him hiking up the mountain and standing in front of Sipi Falls.

Dr. Wheeler searched for Sipi Falls in another browser window. After a moment, the map showed the location up on the side of Mt. Elgon.

Dr. Gonzalez frowned. "Oh, my."

Dr. Wheeler stood up and walked around the conference table, moved a chair, and leaned against the table beside Olivia. He put a hand on her shoulder. "Listen, the world is full of infectious diseases. We talked about those before Eeyore showed up." Dr. Wheeler glanced at Dr. Gonzalez for emphasis. He then looked back at Olivia. "You know as well as I do, the chances of Austin catching anything like this in Africa are almost zero." He turned to Gonzalez. "That was two deaths in—what, five cases—since 1980, right?"

"Right," Gonzalez confirmed.

Looking back at Olivia, Dr. Wheeler asked, "Do you have any idea how many people go up that mountain for camping and whatnot? Do you know how many coffee farmers or goat herders or whatever live on that mountain?"

"No."

"Neither do I, but I'll bet it's a bunch. And if you think about all the people who go up there every year for all these years, and only two of them came down with Marburg, I'd say the odds are way in your favor that nothing bad will happen to your brother. Hell, there's never been any proof they got infected with a rare Filovirus on that mountain. At this point, Mt. Elgon is only a coincidence in those two men's lives."

Olivia looked up at Dr. Wheeler. "I'm sure you're right."

Chapter 34

Everything ached. Austin didn't know if it was the Ebola, the work, or both. He stepped around Nurse Mary-Margaret's blood-soaked body with a bucket in each hand. She'd been lying there all night. They could've had Austin and Littlefield carry the body out but leaving the body there sent a strong unspoken message.

Austin went out through the back door. One of the yellow HAZMAT guys with one hand lazily resting on his weapon stood about ten paces behind the building and watched Austin. Austin breathed in deeply through his surgical mask. There was a time when it had smelled fresh, but so much stink had coated the mask that every breath, whether inside or outside, smelled and tasted the same.

Austin nodded a greeting at the yellow clad Arab, a way to silently say, *I'm friendly. Please don't shoot me.* Not that it mattered. The more Austin saw the people inside suffer, the less he wanted any part of it. Perhaps a bullet was the merciful path to whatever came next.

The guard didn't react to Austin's nod. No surprise. He hadn't responded to Austin, even once, through the course of the night. Austin suspected the guard didn't see him as human, or didn't *want* to see him that way. Seeing him as human would make it harder to kill him. In a way, Austin's nod was a lottery ticket of hope in case the disease didn't do him in. Each nod was a purchase. Maybe one would pay off.

Austin rounded the corner of the building and walked over to the pit, which was situated far enough from the back of the building that the contents could be burned. At least that was Dr. Littlefield's plan. Austin doubted that was going to happen. He dumped the buckets one at a time, careful to do it slowly, lest coagulating lumps drop into the muddy liquid and splash up in his face. When he turned around to head back, he saw the second guard—the one whose job it was to keep an eye on the pit and anyone who came out to dump a body or other waste.

But the guard wasn't standing. He was sitting with his back to the wall and his AK-47 across his lap, resting beneath limp hands.

Austin's first thought was that the guard was dead, but that made no sense at all. How would that have happened? Austin looked to his left. The first guard was out of sight. He looked back at the second. Was the guard asleep?

That was more than possible. It was probable. Austin felt sure that if he sat down, it would only be a matter of seconds before unconsciousness set in. Could it be that much different for the guard? How many hours had they all been on their feet?

But what to do? Walk over to the guard? Say something to see if he was asleep and chance waking him? Put all his chips on the guess that the guard might be sleeping and run for the tree line?

Austin looked left again. The longer he stayed out back, the more likely it was that the other guard would come around the corner to see what was going on.

Austin thought about what he knew and what he didn't know, and it all came down to one thing. His odds of surviving Ebola were maybe as low as ten percent. He recalled what Najid's man had done to Nurse Mary-Margaret, and though he had no idea why Najid hadn't just killed them all—driven by whatever was driving him—he felt sure that his odds of living past his usefulness to Najid were zero.

Ten percent seemed huge compared to zero. So, with

buckets in hand, Austin shuffled toward the tree line. He hoped that a shuffle would earn him a warning from the guard instead of a bullet, if it turned out the guard was awake. The guard didn't move, not in the slightest. Austin shuffled faster.

When the trees were just a step or two to his right, Austin quietly sat the empty buckets on the ground. The guard did not react, so Austin ran for the trees, crashed past some bushes, and nothing happened. No gunshots followed him.

Out of breath and weak — whatever he was infected with stole his stamina — he tore off his mask so he could breathe. After a moment, he ran.

With the fever and the fatigue, Austin couldn't sustain a running pace. Within a few hundred yards, he was jogging and feeling enough pain with each step that he might have stopped had he not been sure that angry men with machine guns would soon be on his heels.

He came to a fork in the trail. The path to the right led down the hill and eventually to a speck of a village called Chebonet. The left led up the mountain. There was one thing he could be sure of. Once the guys in yellow Tyvek suits realized he was gone, he wouldn't be able to outrun them. He'd have to outsmart them.

Putting himself in their shoes, he guessed they'd follow the downward path, thinking that he'd do the same. After all, no one in Austin's condition, even acclimated to an elevation of six thousand feet, would make the choice to head up a path toward Mt. Elgon's crater, fourteen thousand feet up from sea level.

Austin trudged on, thinking of alerting the authorities and trying to figure out how he was going to do that. His phone was crushed. If only he still had that. From up on the mountain he could have picked up a signal from one of the cell towers down in Mbale. He realized he was walking and dragging the toes of his shoes with each step. Setting thoughts of alerting anyone aside, he breathed deeply, painfully, and focused on moving forward, escaping.

Chapter 35

He'd been off the path for a few hours. Running, by that time, was an activity he only aspired to. Even walking fast was too much of an effort. He managed to work his way through the dense forest slowly, the only speed at which it could be transited. That took the running advantage away from his pursuers. So, doing his best to keep quiet, he kept going up, driving himself on through the power of a single hope, that he was outsmarting Najid's HAZMAT guys.

Austin became confused as he climbed the forested slope, working his way around trees as tall as buildings, with trunks as wide as cars, brushing away nettles that stung his skin, staying off the game trails that always looked like the easier path. He was sweating. He was dizzy. No matter how rapidly he breathed, he couldn't get enough air.

Thankfully, he came to a place where the trees grew sparse and the ground leveled. He found himself walking down a row of cultivated plants, waist-high on both sides. The sun was up in the late morning sky, and though a cold breeze was blowing, sweat was rolling down his face and stinging his eyes.

Austin tripped and landed face first in the dirt. In his mind he knew he had to keep going. But when he stood, the mountain was gone. Instead, he looked down a long lush slope and out onto a plain far below, checkered with cultivated fields, speckled with green copses, and veined with rivers.

Where did the mountain go?

In his confusion, he slowly spun around and saw the mountain again. He pushed himself to move, only making it a few more steps before everything went black.

Chapter 36

Eight men — men just like himself, Salim assumed — were in the van already. By the time the van had stopped at two more corners and picked up four more men, Salim dozed off, hypnotized by the hum of the engine beneath his seat.

When he awoke again, they were so far out of the city that the paved highway had turned to dirt. The sun was up and shining brightly through the van. Salim's head bounced against his window as he thought about the map of Kenya he'd seen on the airplane. Nairobi was in the south central part of the country. To the east and north of the capital was the Rift Valley. He didn't know much of anything else about Kenya, except for the fact that it was a popular place for safaris, mostly of the photographic type. He'd seen countless allusions to the Rift Valley and its abundant wildlife while channel surfing late at night back when finding something to watch among a few hundred cable television channels had been his biggest problem.

As the morning wore on, the van passed through ever-shrinking towns, over rougher and rougher roads. Great swaths of farmland spread out in all directions. And eventually a lone mountain rose up out of the horizon until it dominated the western view.

A few times when they were in some deserted part of the road, the van pulled over. The men relieved themselves in the bushes and walked around to stretch. Among them, there were a few whispers between men who seemed to know one another. Beyond that, there was no talking.

Late in the morning, they were fed a simple meal of sun-dried fruits and nuts. But never a word was said about where they were going, how long it would take, or what they would do when they got there. The men were all heading into ambiguity, based on nothing more than faith in their god and their masters.

It was when they were driving north, with the big mountain's thickly-jungled slopes on the left, that the van took a sudden turn onto a narrow path of a road squeezed between the trees and bushes. For five or six miles the van lumbered over rough rocks and large holes, while branches screeched across the paint.

When they'd zigzagged five hundred or a thousand feet up the slope, the van came to the end of the road. Three other safari vans were already parked there, all empty. Waiting in the shade by the vehicles were two menacing men armed with the very familiar AK-47s.

Everybody got out of the safari van. The driver and his partner removed their own AK-47s from luggage bins. Instructions were passed. *Drink if you need it. Relieve yourself if you need to. Prepare to hike.*

Salim wandered around the clearing, getting the knots out of his muscles after so many hours spent sitting numbly, drooling in his sleep, with his head banging against the side window. He breathed deeply of the cool thin mountain air and found himself walking up next to Jalal, who'd perched himself on the edge of a drop off with a view between the crowns of trees. Twenty, or fifty, or maybe a hundred miles across the plain, a mountain of clouds was building, stretching to the horizon while pouring rain and lightening into the black shadow below.

Absently, Jalal said, "It's beautiful."

Though Jalal wasn't looking, Salim nodded. "It reminds me of home."

After a moment, Jalal asked, "The forests in Colorado are this lush?"

"The trees are different, but the mountains are the same. Whenever I stand on one and look down on the world, it takes my breath away."

Jalal turned with a smile. "I never thought of you as the poetic type."

Salim shrugged. "I'm in a weird mood."

Other men shuffled in the dirt and the weeds around the vans. A few found places far enough away for private conversation but with a view of the storm over the plain far to the east.

Salim asked, "Do you ever feel like you're a pawn?"

"A pawn? You slipped pretty quickly from poetic to trite." Jalal smiled at Salim.

"You know what I mean."

"I've felt that way my whole life," Jalal agreed.

Nodding for emphasis, Salim said, "I thought all this would be different."

"How so?"

"I thought maybe I'd feel like somebody. Maybe I thought I'd feel like I was doing something important, making choices, maybe even changing the world."

Jalal laughed. "That's what we're doing, mate. We're going to change the world."

"Into what?"

That confused Jalal. "Into what? What do you mean?"

Salim looked around to make sure no one could hear what he was about to say. "What if it's the same thing?"

"How do you mean?"

"What if we're still powerless, invisible, disposable people, making greedy men more powerful?"

Jalal shook his head and watched the clouds grow and

change. "You think too much, mate."

One of the men in charge called to get everyone's attention, pointed at a trailhead, and told them to get going. Everyone moved in that direction. Salim fell in line as they all headed out on foot along a trail that ran across the slope.

Chapter 37

Emmanuel Muhangi was surprised when he saw Austin stumble, then fall in his coffee field. Not being an excitable type, he squatted in front of his small house and watched for a moment, but Austin never got back up.

It wasn't until his seven-year-old son—who recognized Austin from previous visits—asked why Austin had fallen. It was then that Emmanuel decided to get up and investigate.

After crossing his coffee field, he found Austin—not just fallen, but fainted. Emmanuel shook him but was unable to wake Austin. Upon turning Austin over, he felt his skin, which was burning hot with fever. He'd vomited on himself.

Emmanuel turned to his son and told him to quickly go back to the house and get Emmanuel's wife. Emmanuel, wire-thin but strong from hoisting heavy bags of coffee onto his shoulders, lifted Austin in much the same fashion. He carried Austin to the shed where he and the other mzungu kids slept during their visits.

Emmanuel's wife came in with a bucket of water and some cloths. His daughter was right behind her. They both went to work dabbing the cold water on Austin's skin with the cloths and squeezing dribbles into his mouth.

It was obvious to Emmanuel that Austin was very sick. Sick beyond his wife's abilities to nurse him back to health. After much discussion, Emmanuel left his wife and children with the sick young man and took off at a run down the path that led to Kapchorwa and the closest hospital.

Chapter 38

The trailhead was deceptive. It started out running on a level path across the slope of the mountain. Around a bend it turned upward and forced the group of Pakistani-trained jihadists to hike uphill through the middle of the day. By the time the troop of hikers crested a rise and started to head back down in earnest, they were sweating, thirsty, and spread over a quarter of a mile of the trail.

Salim, walking beside Jalal, could see a group of three about forty or fifty meters ahead. The pair behind was at least that far back.

"What do you think?" Jalal asked.

Salim looked around. "About?"

"This bloody hike through the mountains."

"I'm tired."

"No, mate." Jalal shoved Salim playfully. "You're so morose. Do you think they're going to hide us up here?"

Salim thought for a moment. "They could have put us in any one of those thousand isolated houses we saw on the way out here. Why hide us on the mountain in the forest?"

"It doesn't make any sense to me," Jalal admitted.

"And why did we leave the buses? Why are we walking?" Salim's doubts were overtaking him again. He looked over his shoulder to see how close the nearest followers were. "For as long as we drove this morning, I wonder if we're crossing the border."

"Which border?"

"I'm guessing Uganda," replied Salim.

"Why smuggle ourselves across? We have our passports."

"It makes no sense to me." Salim lowered his voice. "If our passports show that we've entered Kenya, they'll look suspicious if we leave Africa from another country without a stamp for entering that country."

"Unless they're planning an operation in Uganda."

Salim shook his head. "That doesn't make any sense either."

"Why not?"

"If they wanted to hit something in Uganda, why bring us?"

Jalal looked around. "Mate, I don't know how special you think we are, but you do know what we signed up for, right?"

"They could send anybody to Uganda. It's easy to get fighters here. I'll bet they even have training camps in Africa." Salim pointed to the group of three ahead of them. "Those ones are German."

"Germans? How do you know?"

"I heard them speaking German this morning when we first stopped. I heard some other guy speaking English."

"British or American?"

"American," Salim said in a low voice. "I think we all hold Western passports. If that's the case, why send us to Africa? We'd be so much more valuable to the movement if they sent us back to our countries."

"That's what I figured they were planning all along. To send us back."

"Right? So why drag us through the jungle into Uganda? It doesn't make any sense."

Jalal looked around as though there might be some answer in the trees that wasn't readily apparent. "No, mate. It doesn't make any sense."

As the troop made their way down the slope, they eventually closed ranks. They came to a dirt road where a big Isuzu farm truck was waiting for them to load themselves up before heading west once again.

Chapter 39

In the late afternoon sun, Salim leaned over the side of the truck and saw tin roofs and a widening in the dirt road up ahead. A town, a small town. The truck rolled past several men with automatic weapons standing in the bushes. More men were in a position in the trees on the opposite side of the road, looking in the direction from which they'd come. They were guarding the road against anyone coming into town. Salim looked at Jalal with a question on his face, but Jalal was bored and staring at the floor. He never even saw the men guarding the road.

Whatever was happening, they were close to finding out something. Salim was sure of that.

The truck came to a stop and a cloud of red dust billowed around, dropping another layer on them as they coughed. The driver killed the engine, got out, and closed the door. The driver and his passenger came to the back of the truck. The passenger—the man in charge—held up a hand as some of the men in the truck started to get up. "Wait here," he said.

Salim slumped back against the side of the truck. A few of the dust-covered men shared a look. They weren't pleased. Salim wasn't the only one whose curiosity was grating at his patience. The rest of the men kept their feelings more hidden.

Another half-hour passed with the men waiting. They shuffled in their seats. They looked around. They passed silent questions with their eyes.

"Assalamu alaykum."

Salim looked toward the voice, a new man was standing on the ground at the back of the truck.

He said, "Each of you has completed your training."

The speaker's face was covered, whether to keep his identity secret or the road dust off, Salim could only guess.

"You will return to your home countries in the West. You will receive instructions on the way."

Salim looked quickly to the sky and thanked Allah.

"Before you return, you need a cover story. You may be required to explain your absence from your Western lives. Your story will be that you lent humanitarian assistance to the people in this village who are in the midst of a typhoid epidemic. Do not drink the local water."

The speaking man held up a plastic water bottle, the kind that Salim hadn't seen since before boarding the last plane to Lahore a few months prior. "Drink only from the bottles provided, or you will get sick. You will see men in protective suits. Do not speak to them. They are from international aid agencies. They are afraid of typhoid. You should not be. You will be photographed helping these people so that evidence exists of your work here. When you return to your countries, the pictures will be provided to you. You will need to post them on your social media pages to build your story. You will be notified when to start doing this."

Salim smiled inside. Helping sick people in Africa was a great cover to explain his absence over the past months. He might be able to make his escape back into American society without having to go to the FBI. Perhaps an anonymous life somewhere far away from his family in Denver, maybe under a new name, would be the key to getting his freedom back and putting this mistake behind him.

"Each of you will be assigned to a squad," the man behind the truck said. "Your squad leader will tell you what to do. Listen. Do *exactly* as he instructs. One last thing—typhoid can successfully be treated for those who will accept medical treatment early. These people have gone without treatment for several weeks. Many of them are dying. Typhoid is an ugly disease at its end. Some of these people can be saved, but for the rest, your help will make their passing easier."

The speaker pointed at the four men nearest the back of the truck. "You four, come with me."

The man who had been a passenger in the truck selected four other men from the truck to follow him. Soon Salim and Jalal were included in a group of four and following a gruff man with a smelly, matted beard into the village.

Chapter 40

When Austin woke, he heard men's voices nearby and felt the most wonderful cold water on his skin. He was lying on a bed of something soft and looking up at a familiar dark ceiling, though he couldn't quite figure out where he was.

Two kids were speaking in a language he was familiar with, but didn't understand. He noticed his friend Emmanuel's wife looking down over him, pressing a wet cloth against his face.

She said, "Drink."

Austin tried to lift himself up on an elbow, and she leaned over to assist. One of the children brought a cup to his mouth. He drank. When the cup was empty, Austin asked for more, but his stomach roiled. He rolled away from Emmanuel's wife and threw up most of the water onto the dirt floor.

The boy made a noise to express his disgust and his feet shuffled away as Austin laid back. Austin weakly said, "Sorry."

The children both ran outside.

Emmanuel's wife urged him to sit back up. Austin scolded himself for not remembering her name, but it was an African name and had too many syllables and way too many consonants. "Take water again. A little." She held the cup to his mouth. Austin sipped and laid back.

He felt dizzy. He felt confused. He stank badly enough to smell himself. Every part of him ached—his joints, his back, and mostly his head. He lolled his head over to the side to look at Emmanuel's wife on her knees beside him. "Thanks."

She smiled. A closed-lipped smile at first, then a broad smile that showed her perfect white teeth. The oddest thought crossed Austin's mind—that a diet rich in natural, unprocessed foods must be excellent for dental hygiene. They all had great teeth here.

He rolled to his left as another wave of nausea threatened to spill his last sips of water into the dirt.

Emmanuel's wife made a soothing sound—the kind that mothers instinctively make when caring for sick children—then dipped the cloth back into the bucket and rubbed it over his face, arms, and neck.

The sound of the children's voices outside changed. Deeper voices joined them. Emmanuel's familiar voice said something to his son.

Feet shuffled through dirt, and bodies brushed through the shed's narrow door. Then voices were inside and Austin opened his eyes to see two men in yellow Tyvek suits with AK-47s in their hands. They stood over him, hunched down under the shed's low roof.

Austin closed his eyes and waited for the bullet.

Chapter 41

Her mother was an Olympic silver medalist. And every time Eric brought it up in front of strangers in the cafeteria, she wanted to take her tray and smack him in the head hard enough to make his thick, red hair pop right off his head. But she didn't, of course. Instead, she smiled and looked at the disbelief around the table. Nobody ever believed it.

"No," Eric's old friend Robert said.

Olivia nodded to confirm and continued to chew her food.

Robert asked, "So your mother is really a Russian Olympic medalist?"

Olivia swallowed, took her billfold out of her purse, opened it up to the pictures she had saved inside, and laid it on the table for everyone to see.

Eric had seen it before and took the opportunity to shovel food into his mouth. He had to shovel. He had such a mound on his tray that if he ate at a normal pace, he wouldn't finish before their lunch break was over. Olivia couldn't figure out why he wasn't obese.

She flipped the photos in their little clear plastic sleeves. She found the old one of her mother on the platform, hands raised, and a medal around her neck.

Robert—without asking—reached out and scooted the wallet closer. He leaned over as did his coworker Joan. "She's gorgeous," Robert said.

That wasn't unexpected. Olivia had heard the comment too many times for it to have any impact.

Joan was a little more catty. "I was expecting—"

Of course, she didn't finish. Everyone expected female

Russian athletes from the mid-eighties to look like brutish men full of growth hormones. Olivia's mother was nothing like that. If she'd been taller, she'd have looked like one of those magazine cover models.

"What did she earn a medal in?" Robert asked with a vaguely lustful look in his eyes, glancing first at the photograph, and then over to Olivia. There was a strong resemblance between the two, though Olivia thought she had nothing close to her mother's beauty.

"Biathlon," Olivia answered.

"You have her eyes," Robert said. It was what guys always said when they saw a picture of her mother. It probably wasn't even true. What Olivia thought it meant was, "I want to have sex with you and pretend you are your mother." Comments about her eyes never got guys very far with her.

"I don't watch the Winter Olympics," Joan told the table, "What's a biathlon?"

"Skiing and shooting."

"Skiing and shooting?" Joan laughed. "Are you kidding? In the same event?"

Olivia often wondered what it was about most Americans that made them so laughably proud of their ignorance of any sport that wasn't American-style football. "Google it." She took another bite of her salad and thought again about smacking Eric with the tray.

"So, is your father Russian, too?" Robert asked.

"American, I guess." Olivia answered.

Idly, Robert added, "My dad's from Iowa. His family was surprised when he married a girl from Michigan."

Everyone laughed politely.

"So," Robert turned his attention back to Olivia, "Your

mom is Russian, your dad is American. Did you grow up in the States?"

"Some," Olivia answered. "I was born in Texas."

"Texas?" Joan asked. "I'm from Midland."

"We moved to Pakistan when I was little. We lived in Islamabad until I was thirteen. Then we came back to the US. I've been here ever since."

"So you learned Russian from your mother?"

Olivia nodded. Her reputation for languages was something Eric also bragged about.

"And Pakistani?" He asked.

"Urdu," Olivia nodded. "I also speak Punjabi, Pashto, and obviously, English."

"Jesus."

Olivia shrugged. The languages had always been easy.

Robert said, "All the languages I know are things like SQL, Java, C++, stuff like that."

"And English." Eric laughed again, but the others only smiled.

"Are you in IT, also?" Olivia asked Joan.

"Project manager," Joan confirmed. "How long have you worked with Eric?"

"Worked *for* him," Olivia smiled.

"Oh, yeah," Robert exaggerated, "Eric's a manager now. I keep forgetting."

"A year," Olivia answered.

"Before that?" Robert asked.

"I've been with the agency since I finished grad school."

"So the NSA is your first job?"

"Yes."

"Oh, God," Robert laughed, "Well, start working on

your resumé, or you'll end up like him. He looks like he's forty, but he's only been here a few more years than you."

More laughs.

Thankfully, the rest of the lunch conversation centered around Joan's teenagers and Eric's toddlers.

After they finished eating, Joan and Robert walked together down a hallway that led to the IT sections of the building. Eric badged in at the elevator, and when they were inside, badged again to access the third floor where both he and Olivia worked.

"What's that thing you were working on before lunch?" Eric asked, "How's that going?"

"With Salim Pitafi?" Olivia answered.

"Is that his name? Pitafi? The one from Denver."

"Yes. He was passed to us by Harvey Singleton's group. For a few years now he's been taking an interest in radical Muslim websites. When he bought a ticket to Pakistan, he fell into our lap."

"You've been monitoring him?" Eric asked.

The elevator door opened and both Eric and Olivia stopped talking. Eric directed Olivia to one of the dozens of glass-walled conference rooms situated around the edges of the cubicle farm. Once inside, they pulled up chairs across from one another at a small table.

Olivia said, "Once he landed in Lahore, he disappeared. Not a trace of him came up anywhere for three months."

"Training camp?" Eric asked.

Olivia wasn't ready to make that call for certain so she went through her analysis. "No debit card usage that I could find. Not a single phone call. His phone is still active on his parent's account, but it's been dead. He has relatives in Multan—that's where his family is from."

"First generation?"

"He was born in Multan," said Olivia. "His parents immigrated to the US when he was young. He was three or four at the time."

"So he's been here all his life?"

Olivia nodded. "For all practical purposes."

"In the same place?"

"In Denver," she answered.

Eric asked, "And he flew out of Lahore yesterday?"

"A little after noon, local time."

"Destination?"

"Nairobi," she said.

"Nairobi? So maybe he was visiting relatives in Multan, and decided to go see elephants and giraffes?" Eric guessed.

"You know that's unlikely."

"I'm playing devil's advocate," Eric said. "Tell me why I'm wrong."

Olivia didn't take offense. Questions were part of the analytical process. "If this was truly a social visit to Multan, then why the silence? He didn't use his phone. He didn't post any pictures to his Facebook account. He didn't log into any computer under his name or an alias that we're aware of."

"And he would have posted something?" Eric asked.

"He was an active Facebook user until about three or four months before he flew to Lahore. He posted pictures of ski trips, hiking trips, whatever. He even posted pictures of him and his buddies at the Denver Zoo."

"When?" Eric asked.

"Six months before leaving," Olivia said. "He was

skipping classes at the local community college." She didn't mention that the community college was just fifteen minutes from her dad's house. That detail wasn't important, and it wasn't relevant. It was only disturbing because the jihadist had lived relatively close to her father.

"Maybe he just got tired of Facebook."

"Safari tours in Kenya are expensive," said Olivia. "His family here in the US doesn't have any money. At least, not the kind of money to finance a globe-hopping tour for their son. In addition to Salim, they've got two other kids nearing college age. They've got too much credit card debt and payments on two fairly new cars. They live paycheck to paycheck."

Eric sat back in his chair and thought for a moment. "So the kid spent a lot of time surfing jihadist websites prior to dropping out of sight for a visit to Pakistan three months ago. Now he's traveling around South Central Asia and Africa with no apparent way to pay for it. And we don't know why. Are the parents in communication with the kid at all?"

Shaking her head, Olivia said, "Not a peep since he left."

"Okay. I'll send it up the chain and see how they want to proceed."

"What do you think will happen?" Olivia asked.

"I don't know. They may send the FBI out to talk to the parents to see what's up. They may put them under surveillance. Why don't you keep working this and see what else comes out?"

Olivia said, "Something else already did."

"What's that?"

"Two other names popped up when I started looking before lunch. Both Pakistani-Americans, both took an interest in radical websites, both disappeared to Pakistan."

"At the same time?" Eric was interested.

"One took off a month before. One took off a few weeks after."

"Tell me about those two."

Olivia said, "Both are en route to Nairobi or already there."

"No shit."

Olivia nodded. Her face was serious.

"Do we have any reason to believe these guys know each other?" Eric asked.

"None. They didn't even take the same flights."

"All right," Eric paused for a moment. "Send me those names when you get back to your desk. I'm going to tell Barry Middleton to drop what he's doing and lend you a hand."

"I don't know if I need help yet."

"He has extensive experience with different types of data. Bring him up to speed. I want regular updates on this. I'm going to send the info upstairs."

They were on the third floor of a three-story building. Olivia understood what *upstairs* meant. "You think there's something going on?"

Eric nodded.

Chapter 42

When Austin woke, he was lying on his side on a cot. Everything was still confusing, and thoughts were hard to string together through the fog and gaps in his brain. How long had he been out? Hours? A day or two? More?

One of the plastic buckets that he'd become so familiar with over the past days sat on the floor not ten inches from his head. It stank. The cot stank. The room stank.

On the other side of the bucket, on the floor, Margaux lay on her side facing him. Her face was slack, her eyes open—blood-red, not focused. They were doll's eyes, horrible for their lifelessness. Her mouth dripped a brownish mucus—the remains of her last regurgitation. Except for the twitching of two fingers on the hand that lay by her face, she looked dead.

On Margaux's other side, a young African woman was sprawled, with blackish red blood smeared on her face. A trickle of blood ran from her ear down to the floor where her head lay, well off her mat. One of her arms was resting across Margaux. The woman's fingers were curled back over her palms, pulled closed by dead tendons. The woman's chest didn't rise, nor did it fall. There was no breath in her. Only the flies on her skin were alive, animated in hunger for her remains.

The absence of Benoit on a mat at Margaux's side put a clear and certain thought into Austin's mind. Benoit was dead. That meant his body was piled by the waste pit behind the hospital, waiting for somebody with enough commitment and energy to burn it.

A tear rolled out of Austin's eye and tracked across the bridge of his nose, down the slope on the other side and across his cheek. The pain of Benoit's death, mixed with all the other agony trapped in the confines of his skin, seemed too much to bear. And in moments of clarity, Austin knew the pain that lived behind the sallow, dejected eyes of all those third-world children on all those television commercials that begged for his latte money when he was back in Denver. With the pain branded so deeply on his own soul, he'd never look at those eyes again and keep his tears to himself.

In the next moment of lucidity, he recalled the prognosis of his predicament. Benoit was dead. Margaux was dying. Austin would soon see them on the other side and never again have to look at diseased children with big eyes and distended bellies.

It occurred to Austin in that moment that he should be dead already.

Austin felt the weight of someone sitting down behind him on the cot. With all the slow care he could use to keep his stomach from spewing whatever remained there, he rolled onto his back. One of the guys in yellow Tyvek was sitting beside him, looking down.

Through the goggles Austin saw medium brown skin, black eyebrows, and familiar black eyes. "Rashid?"

"You are Austin." It wasn't Rashid's voice, but his brother's older, harsher voice.

"Najid?" Austin asked. "Why?"

"You did me a kindness."

Austin was confused. He was asking why Najid was in Kapchorwa with gunmen, why he'd killed Nurse Mary-Margaret—not for a moment of warm, fuzzy emotional shit. What the hell was he doing?

Najid said, "You are a friend of Rashid's. You telephoned

me out of concern for him. I returned the kindness by not having you killed."

Austin tried to put the words "fuck you" together, but was having trouble getting his mouth to cooperate.

"Not that it matters. You'll soon be dead I suspect. It seems that nearly all who are in the advanced stages of the disease are dying."

Austin looked to his left to see the ward.

Guessing the question, Najid answered in a detached voice. "Forty-eight so far." He looked to the other end of the ward. "The doctor says another ten or twelve will go within the hour."

To his right, Austin saw Rashid lying on the cot next to his. A HAZMAT guy — the doctor, Austin guessed — sat beside Rashid doing some kind of exam.

Najid's voice grew sad, and he shook his head. "Rashid has a better chance than the rest of you. He is getting the best medical treatment available under the circumstances."

"But—" That was the entirety of the question Austin had the energy to put together.

"It's not fair?" Najid shook his head, exaggerating the gesture. "No, it's *not* fair. Rashid gets care that will double or triple his chances of surviving, and you—" Najid paused, "lying right next to him, in fact, lying right next to a box that contains enough drugs to treat you and maybe a dozen others—get nothing. Do know why?"

Because you're a piece of shit. But those words couldn't find a voice either.

"That is exactly what is going on now. American doctors with Ebola have been flown out of Liberia and are responding well to a new American miracle drug. The supply is small and the price is high. So poor Africans don't get it. They die. That is the world, Austin. You don't understand it because you have been a rich American all your life, and you have had more of everything than you ever needed, while others suffered to provide it for you. At this moment, that is no longer the case. Rashid has more drugs to treat this disease than he will ever need. And you have nothing. The sadness of the world's reality looks different from this perspective, doesn't it?"

Austin slowly shook his head.

Najid laid a gloved hand on Austin's arm. "I know you will not believe this, but I do hope you live. That is why I had my men carry you off the mountain. Do not run again. Our activities here must be kept secret and the value of the kindness you showed does not compare to that need." Najid took his hand off Austin's arm, turned to the doctor in the yellow Tyvek suit, and started speaking in Arabic.

Chapter 43

"Will he live?" Najid asked the doctor, using the convenience of his native tongue to hide the conversation from Austin.

"There is no way to tell. I do all that I can. There is no cure for Ebola, you know that." Dr. Kassis stood up, took a syringe, and injected some medicine into Rashid's IV. "All I can do is treat the symptoms and try to keep the symptoms from killing him."

"What is that drug you just injected?"

"It is an anticoagulant," replied the doctor.

"An anticoagulant? That does not make sense to me. It is my understanding that hemorrhagic fever causes one to bleed until he dies."

"Yes, but it is more complex than that."

"How so?" Najid leaned forward. He needed to know as much as he could about the disease he was hoping to unleash on the West.

Dr. Kassis sat back down. Without waking Rashid, he checked his temperature with an infrared scanning thermometer. "The process is complex. In the early phases of the disease, blood clots form and float freely in the bloodstream. These clots clump together and clog small veins."

"Like a stroke?" Najid asked.

"Exactly like a stroke. That explains the dementia symptoms we see in Ebola and Marburg patients. Parts of the brain are deprived of oxygen and cease to function correctly. When the oxygen supply is cut off for too long, that part of the brain dies."

Najid shook his head and laid a gloved hand across

Rashid's forehead.

"Just as importantly, the clots form in the liver, the kidneys, the lungs, the intestines—all of the organs, even the heart."

Najid nodded. "That is why you give him the anticoagulant, to stop that process?"

"Exactly right." Kassis said. "If we can stop the clotting, we have a chance when we reach the next phase of the disease."

"The bleeding?" Najid asked.

"Yes. The bleeding occurs because the blood has run out of coagulants. That coincides with tissue death all over the body. Where the tissue has died, eventually it bleeds."

"Everywhere," Najid concluded.

"Yes. Everywhere. It flows from every orifice, catastrophically. However, if we can use the anticoagulants to limit the damage from the clotting, we can later use coagulants to limit the bleeding. We keep him hydrated in the mean time and hope what we are doing helps."

"So, anticoagulants to reduce the damage, and later coagulants to keep him from dying," Najid summarized, more to get it straight in his own mind than to let Dr. Kassis know he understood.

"Yes," replied Kassis.

"How do you know when to stop using one and start using the other?"

"That is my job, Najid."

"I trust your judgment." Najid looked down for a long time at his brother, imagining the sorrow his father would feel to lose him. It would be worse because his father was the one who had forced Rashid to spend his summer in Africa, seeing what life looked like from the other side.

"When Ebola has spread the world over, do you have a plan for how we will survive?" Dr. Kassis asked.

Najid looked up at the doctor. "The Western countries will develop a vaccine or an effective treatment. They have the technology and the experience. As we discussed, it is only a matter of time. When that time comes, we will buy enough for ourselves."

Dr. Kassis raised an eyebrow, hidden under his goggles. "And if the Americans won't sell it?"

"The Americans likely won't, but I am converting my father's fortune to gold. There will never be a time in this world when I won't be able to find a man willing to sell his soul for a handful of gold."

"Gold? How so?"

"I have instructed our man in Switzerland to sell everything, purchase gold bullion, and have it shipped to my father's compound within the next few days. Gold will be the only currency with value when the world economies fall apart. My family may come out of this as the wealthiest on the planet. I have little doubt that I can pay corrupt Americans for all we need."

Dr. Kassis adjusted his mask. It was becoming a habit, along with the fear of not knowing which was worse, an ill fitting mask, or a snug mask being touched by contaminated hands. "It is possible that gold will be worthless? It may be that only bullets, water, and food will have value."

Najid laughed out loud. "Your faith in men runs deeper than mine, doctor. In all of man's history, except for the age of electronics, gold has never had any intrinsic value. At best it was made into trinkets that didn't rust. But men have always traded weapons, water, food, even their lives to possess it. It will be so in the future. The value men place on gold has never been rational. So it will continue."

"Wiser than proceeding down this road with only a hope for a cure would be to have a backup plan." Dr. Kassis laid a gloved palm across Rashid's forehead. "I will speak candidly."

"Of course."

Dr. Kassis turned to face Najid. "In case I fall ill and am unable to offer it at a later date, I wish to tell you now?"

Najid scrutinized the doctor. "Do you think you might fall ill?"

"I don't know. The risk is great. Our clean room is not so clean. I don't know whether every man follows the procedures as required. It only takes one lazy man failing to remove a bit of contaminated protective gear for all of us to become infected."

Najid's anger rose. "Have you seen someone do this?"

"No," Dr. Kassis shook his head slowly, showing his fatigue. "When men get tired, they make mistakes. That is all I am saying."

"If one has made a mistake and we become infected, or if we simply aren't protected well enough and we fall ill, what is this alternative?"

"I know you educated yourself a great deal about this disease before we came here. Did you read about the outbreak in Kikwit in 1995?"

"I am not familiar with that outbreak," replied Najid.

"More than three hundred fell ill. Eighty percent died."

"Not as bad as some outbreaks."

"No." Dr. Kassis stood up and stretched. "Let's walk a bit."

Najid stood up and the two men waded through the prone townsfolk, with their distant, empty faces and near-lifeless bodies. They followed the center aisle to the front doors and went out to stand on the patio.

The doctor leaned on the porch railing. "Near the end of the outbreak, one of the nurses fell ill, a Zairian woman. This disturbed the Zairian doctors greatly. They had all been taking precautions, including this nurse. They wore goggles, masks, gloves, and suits. They disinfected themselves with bleach, sprayed it on the suits, and waded through pools of bleach on the way out of the sick wards. All procedures were followed, but still, she fell ill."

"That is a frightening prospect," said Najid.

"For one thing, it tells us how dangerous this disease is. It takes a dozen or fewer virions—"

"Virion? I do not know this word."

"It is an individual virus—a strand of RNA or DNA wrapped in a shell of proteins. An individual package—the infectious particle designed for transmission of any virus is called a virion."

"Interesting that you don't talk as though it is alive."

Dr. Kassis nodded, "Yes, it is good that you caught that. Viruses exist somewhere between living and nonliving things, as we traditionally think of them. The point I'm making, though, is that given the unimaginably tiny amount of material it takes to make up a dozen virions, it takes only the imperceptibly smallest of mistakes to become infected."

"That is not encouraging, Dr. Kassis."

The doctor shook his head. "That is exactly what the Zairian doctors thought. And after seeing one of their own —the nurse—contract the virus, they knew that any one of them might be next. Who can say if it was that, or pure altruism motivating their subsequent choices? Regardless, they took a risk on an experimental treatment."

Najid gave Dr. Kassis his full attention. "What do you know of this experimental treatment?"

"Some of the Ebola patients survived. Indeed, some were on the road to full recovery. They clearly had the antibodies in their blood to fight off the virus. That is how immunity works in humans."

Seemed pretty basic to Najid. "I understand that."

"The risk they took—against the wishes and objections from the American and European doctors—was to transfuse a measure of blood from one of the healthy survivors to the sick nurse."

"What happened?"

"The nurse got better."

Najid stood up straight and couldn't hide the surprise in his voice. "That sounds miraculous."

Nodding, Dr. Kassis said, "The Zairian doctors then tried the same treatment on seven other patients."

"Against the wishes of the Westerners?" Najid asked.

"Yes."

Najid thought for a moment. "Did they survive?"

"All but one of them did."

"In seven out of eight, the treatment worked?" Najid confirmed.

"It *appeared* to have worked," replied Kassis.

"What do you mean by that?"

"The decision to test the new treatment occurred at the end of the outbreak. There was no way to know whether or not the virus had mutated to a less lethal form of itself."

"So no one knew for sure if it was the treatment that cured them."

"No." Dr. Kassis looked at Najid. "There may come a time when we are desperate enough to try this same treatment to save our lives. There may come a time when it is the only hope we have."

"Then save Rashid. If I have to take another's blood in a transfusion, it is Rashid's I'll have."

"Are you of the same blood type?"

"I am."

.

Chapter 44

Salim and Jalal's team of four broke up early in their shift. They'd been carrying bodies out of houses at first, moving them to a shockingly large pile of human remains behind the hospital. They started at one end of town, working their way from house to house. Those who were sick, they helped or carried to the hospital or school.

Most houses had at least one corpse inside, surrounded by wailing family members. At many houses, the residents lied about sick family members. Some resisted physically. But a brandished AK-47 always brought an end to their resistance.

Most of the ailing couldn't make it to a recently opened space in the hospital or school under their own power and had to be carried. In the humidity, heat, and stench, Salim's shoulders, back, and arms cramped from the work. Two months' training in Pakistan had left him in the best shape of his life, but he had found the limits of his physical abilities.

The saddest part of the whole endeavor wasn't even the work. It was the hopelessness, made visceral by the bodies and the smells. Salim had touched the skin of many of the dead. He'd brought hollow comfort to the dying by holding their hands. He saw mothers weeping for dead husbands, children crying over their mothers, and fathers—men with wiry muscles and calloused hands—wailing over their dead children.

When he and Jalal were switched to the water detail, Salim thanked Allah for the change.

Salim was trying to wash the memories of the dying out of his mind with the sound of the water Jalal was pumping into the pails. He watched two men in yellow Tyvek, armed with AK-47s, standing lazily in the middle of the town's only intersection, with red dust covering their feet and fading to orange up around their knees. Other freedom fighters were working their way in and out of houses by then. Some were carrying in water. Some were carrying out buckets. Some were taking out bodies. Some stood around in gaps between the houses, talking and gesturing. Their body language showed their suspicions and fears.

Salim looked around to make sure no one but Jalal was close enough to hear what he was about to say. "It doesn't make any sense."

Jalal pumped the handle to draw more water out of the well. "What doesn't?"

"None of it."

Jalal kept pumping. "That's a broad statement, mate. We're helping these people. That's what they said we'd do. They said it was our cover story. It makes sense." Jalal looked at Salim. "It doesn't to you?"

"Of course it does. It makes fantastic sense." Salim rolled his eyes.

"Sarcasm won't make your point," said Jalal. "Tell me what doesn't make sense."

"Well—" Salim gestured toward the yellow HAZMAT guys.

Jalal shrugged and pumped more water. "What about them?"

"Are you kidding?" Salim asked. "Are *they* with us? They told us when we got off the truck that they were aid workers. Why do they have guns? Why don't they aid anyone?"

Jalal looked at the men in yellow standing with their

guns and doing nothing but looking bored. "They're here for security. You know how these kinds of situations get."

Salim lowered his voice as his impatience rose. "No, Jalal, I don't know how these situations get."

"Well it makes sense that we might need security, right?" Jalal asked.

"Yeah, of course."

"There, then," Jalal concluded.

"Why the yellow suits? Why don't *we* have suits?" Salim asked.

Water sloshed out of the top of one of the water pails as Jalal moved it away from the pump. Jalal pointed to the main hospital building. "That one next."

Salim looked over at the school. "We did all three buildings there. Are we taking anything to the church?"

Jalal laughed quietly, but harshly. "Christians?"

Salim shrugged, and they walked up the dirt road toward the hospital building.

Jalal said, "It's typhoid. We don't need the suits."

"Then why do *they* need them?" asked Salim.

Jalal smiled. "Maybe they're ignorant wankers."

Salim shook his head and walked a bit. "Why *aren't* we boiling the water?"

"Because it would be a lot of trouble." Jalal stopped in the road. Salim stopped and looked at him. Jalal said, "We're drawing water from a well in the middle of Africa, mate. It's probably cleaner than the water we get at home."

"I think typhoid spreads through the water system." Salim told him flatly.

"That's not what I heard," Jalal countered.

"Heard? Heard from whom?"

"I remember from school," said Jalal.

"What do you remember?"

Jalal started to walk forward with his bucket. "I don't know."

Frustrated, Salim asked, "Then why did you say that?"

"What do *you* remember about typhoid from school? Did you take a class in diseases or something?" asked Jalal.

"No, I don't remember where I learned it. I just remember it's a disease that spreads through water."

"Fine. Is it a virus or a bacteria?"

Salim was getting frustrated. "Why are you being such an asshole? I'm not trying to argue with you about something you think you know, but don't. I just want to understand what's going on."

"Take it on faith, Salim."

"What, that you think you know something about typhoid, but don't?"

Jalal shook his head. "It sounds like you don't know anything about typhoid, either. You're stressed and you're trying to think of reasons why you think they're going to screw us. But think about it, mate. Why would they screw us? How could they screw us? We've already promised our lives to the cause. What more could they get out of us?"

Salim shrugged. "I don't know. Have you seen anybody taking pictures of us? Weren't they supposed to be taking pictures of us to post?"

"Just do your work. There are a lot of us here. They'll get to us."

"We've been here for eight hours, at least," replied Salim.

Jalal didn't answer. They climbed the stairs. Salim opened the hospital door and followed Jalal inside.

Jalal took his pail and a metal cup and started on one side of the center aisle. Salim went to work on the other. They stopped by each bed or mat, tried to get the patient to drink, then moved to the next.

By the time Salim had visited ten beds, he'd already come across two patients he was sure were dead. Several were alive but unresponsive. Most of them had blood-red eyes, and some of them had blood on their blankets, clothes, and skin.

About halfway up on his side of the ward, Salim came to a cot that held a young Arab man. He had an IV—the only one Salim had seen. He was clean. He wore blue hospital scrubs—recently washed. His sheets weren't stained in filth. A man in a plastic yellow suit hovered over the young man and waved Salim past.

The next surprise was a pair of Caucasians—a young man on a cot and a woman with absent eyes on a mat on the floor. Salim shuffled up between them, knelt by the familiar-looking young man, shook him awake, and held the cup of water up near his face.

The young man's eyes snapped open. At first, he just stared at the ceiling. Salim helped him to sit up a bit and held the cold cup of water to the boy's lips. But instead of drinking, the boy looked at Salim's face, studied it, and croaked, "Sam?"

In that same second, Salim recognized the boy as Austin Cooper. They'd gone to high school together.

What the hell?

Then the terror set in. It wouldn't go well for him if anyone realized the sick boy knew him. Those in charge would jump to conclusions, and those conclusions would be bad. Salim stood straight up—looking up as he did—and saw the guy in the HAZMAT suit beside the tidy Arab kid's bed staring at him.

Chapter 45

Eric stopped by the conference room. Inside, Olivia Cooper and Barry Middleton shared the desk. The room was bigger than the one Eric and Olivia had occupied earlier in the day. It held an oblong table designed to seat six. In the center of the table sat a conference call phone set and a projector, which at the moment wasn't hooked up to either computer.

Eric dropped himself into a chair and asked, "What do you have?"

Olivia pointed at Barry and said, "Barry got us the lists of passengers on all the flights for the past several days, including Salim's flight."

Eric took a drink of his coffee. "And?"

"I'm working on the information, but it looks like there's been a big spike in passengers flying from Lahore to Nairobi on Western passports."

"A big spike?" replied Eric.

"It seems to have gone up significantly compared to the day before."

Eric shook his head. "By itself, that information is somewhat meaningless."

"Yes," Olivia agreed. "Barry is pulling in information from the past month so we can see how far it deviates from the trend."

Eric shook his head. "Statistical anomalies are interesting, and they may mean something, but you know if you go into a problem with a bias toward finding a certain solution, even in random data, you're going to find a pattern that supports your solution. All you have to do is look long enough." Eric glanced at Barry. "I shouldn't have to tell you that."

Olivia spoke up to pull the attention back to herself. "This isn't all we've found. Thirteen of those Western passport holders are young men from the ages of nineteen to twenty-seven. All left the United States within the past four months."

Eric said, "You have my attention."

"They are all on our list."

In the department, The List didn't need to be named specifically. It was the list they were tasked with monitoring — US citizens who'd gone abroad under suspicious circumstances — those under suspicion of potentially joining an anti-American radical group.

Eric turned to Barry. "You confirmed this?"

Barry nodded. "It gets better."

"How's that?" replied Eric.

Barry pointed at Olivia. "I sent her the info just before you walked in."

Eric turned to Olivia. She was staring wide-eyed at her screen. "Barry?" Her voice was tentative as she glanced sideways at him, then back at her screen. "Tell me I'm understanding this correctly."

"Judging by the look on your face, I'd say you are."

"What?" Eric asked.

Glancing between Barry and her screen, she turned to Eric. "Pass me that cord."

Eric passed her the plug to connect her laptop to the projector. Olivia plugged it into her computer, fiddled with a few keys, and an image of her computer's screen illuminated the wall.

The projected image on the wall contained a spreadsheet with a column of names — some highlighted in yellow — a column of amounts in some currency not relevant at the moment, a couple of date columns, and columns of flight numbers, carriers, flight times, destinations, numbers of stops, what appeared to be account numbers, and a column that seemed to randomly contain the letter W or blanks.

"Sort by column D," Barry told Olivia, as she maneuvered the mouse across the top of the spreadsheet.

Olivia clicked a few menu options, and the information was ready for review. She said, "The rows highlighted in yellow are the thirteen I told you about a moment ago—Americans."

Eric scanned the document, trying to see what was so obvious and important to his two subordinates. "Help me out with this."

Olivia moused over one of the yellow-highlighted names. "This is one of our boys."

Eric read out loud, "Salim Pitafi."

"Look to column D," Olivia moused down the column and highlighted six rows."

"And that column is?" Eric asked.

"The credit card number used to pay for the ticket." Olivia glanced at Barry.

"That's right." Barry was excited. "That column next to it. That's when the purchase was made."

Eric looked at it for a moment. "Are you telling me that all six of those tickets were purchased with the same credit card number at the same time?"

"That's exactly what it says." Olivia scrolled down the page and highlighted contiguous rows, in groups of six. "It happens again and again—nineteen groups of six—all for tickets purchased in a two-hour window."

"Scroll down slowly from the top," Eric requested.

Olivia moved the mouse to the top of the spreadsheet and scrolled.

Barry nodded emphatically after the second yellow highlighted name was passed.

When they got to the bottom, Eric said, "By my count, nine of those grouped purchases contain at least one of the guys on our lists."

"Yes," Olivia answered.

"Exactly." Barry confirmed.

"You think these guys are all related somehow?"

"The accounts prove that," Barry blurted.

Eric turned to Barry, "Yes. No doubt. But what is the relationship? That's the important thing, right? Without a doubt this is compelling, but we don't know if a travel agency is booking these boys on safari on behalf of some university travel abroad program, some church is sending groups of missionaries, or they're part of some elaborate terrorist plot. Am I right?"

Olivia sank in her seat.

Barry flatly replied, "You're right."

"I'm not saying this is or isn't something," Eric told them. "As I said, I'm curious. I'm even suspicious. I've kicked the inquiry about your boy Salim and the other two upstairs. I'll pass along the other ten names. But until we can get more information on what these card numbers relate to, or until we can get some information on who these others are, we can't make an educated guess. We can make a guess, but we have to recognize that's all it is—a guess. As I already mentioned, we're looking for terrorists here. We expect to find them. So every bit of evidence we find is going to smell like terrorist shit. You understand what I'm saying?"

"Yes," Olivia responded.

Barry nodded.

Eric stood up, walked over to the glass door, and pulled it open. He stopped with one foot out. "Both of you — move your stuff to conference room D-3."

Olivia looked across the floor to the line of three large conference rooms on the opposite wall.

"I'm sending Katherine to join you. She'll liaise with our friends at the CIA and see what we can come up with on these other names. Kevin will help you get into the bank information. Christine can dig into the phone data. Save me a place at the table, 'cause I'll be checking up on you guys frequently. We'll order some food in later." Eric walked out and let the door swing closed behind him.

"Holy crap," Barry said.

Olivia smiled, but felt anxious, "I hope I'm not sending everyone off chasing nothing."

"You're doing your job. Eric gets paid to make these calls."

"And if I'm wrong?"

"You're not wrong about anything. We collect data and we analyze it — that's what we do. We dig further into things when they look like they might be important. This *looks* like it might be important. Maybe it is, maybe it isn't. Not every hole you dig has a diamond at the bottom. Eric knows that. We'll just keep pushing on until the data says we have something or we don't." Barry raised an eyebrow and smiled.

Olivia felt no less anxious.

Chapter 46

Najid stepped onto the patio and looked over at the tiny free school halfway between the hospital and the main school. Dr. Kassis had set up a primitive divider with sheets of canvas from a farm truck. He'd doused the whole space with bleach, and it became a clean zone. It was the only place in Kapchorwa where any of them could remove their gear and take care of the body's necessities. The conditions in the schoolhouse weren't much better than the setup for the sick in the hospital or any of the other overflowing buildings. A few cots gave them a place to take turns sleeping. Not that Najid had slept. He'd been on his feet for more hours than he cared to think about, but there would be time for resting and sleeping later.

Nevertheless, Najid was thinking about going to the clean room in the free school, removing his Tyvek suit, gloves, goggles, and mask. It would feel so good to be out of the hot, stinking suit.

The sound of gunfire from the west cut those thoughts short.

Najid ran to one of the Range Rovers as the two men who'd been standing guard in the center of town ran over. Removing an AK-47 from the rear compartment, Najid motioned for the others to get in. He had men stationed a quarter-mile to the west of town who had been tasked to block the road. It wasn't a far run, but driving there would be faster than running and risking overheating in the suits. Najid jumped into the passenger's seat, and one of his other men took the driver's side and started the engine.

Once the other guard got in the back seat, the vehicle started to roll. Another of his men came running up to the vehicle and Najid spoke in rushed Arabic, instructing him to keep the others at their duties in the village. The Land Rover accelerated along the dirt road through the tiny town throwing up a plume of dust. By the time they passed the last house, the gunshots had ceased.

Najid worried about what he'd find when he reached his men at the roadblock. They were not experienced soldiers. They'd been through a month or two of training in Pakistan or Afghanistan, and perhaps even a little extra training in Africa. If there had been a firefight, it had ended quickly, with too few shots. And that was the point that worried him. His men weren't experienced enough to kill armed enemies so quickly.

The road made a sudden, hairpin curve. The driver cornered the Land Rover around the curve and bounced it through a shallow riverbed with the skill of an experienced wadi basher. Najid checked his weapon. The magazine was full. He moved the lever on his AK-47 from safety to semi-auto, the position he preferred when shooting. He put the weapon out of the window and laid the muzzle over the mirror, ready to fire at any threat that materialized ahead.

In the back seat, his man positioned himself in the center, and pointed his muzzle up between the seats and out through the windshield.

The road snaked through a few curves, finally coming to a section that ran straight. Not too far in the distance, a few vehicles sat in the middle of the road.

The driver slowed, and Najid commanded him to stop. He flung his door open, jumped out, and raised his weapon to his shoulder, using the door for whatever cover it provided. The two men with him positioned themselves on the other side of the Land Rover.

A man was jogging up the road toward the SUV before the dust settled around them. He looked like one of the men Najid had positioned at the roadblock. Down along the sights on his rifle, Najid looked past the jogging man. He spotted what looked like a half-dozen people lying on the shoulder. A few armed men were visible around the vehicles and in the trees nearby.

Breathing heavily, the runner coming toward them slowed, and raised his rifle over his head. He wasn't wearing protective gear. None of the men Najid left at the roadblocks wore gear — they were expendable.

Certain of the runner's identity, Najid waved him closer. "Come."

The man hurried over to stand on the other side of the door.

"What happened?" Najid asked.

The runner pointed behind him. "Doctors. Aid workers."

Najid looked at the bodies.

"They are dead." After speaking, the runner focused on Najid's masked face, looking for some reaction.

Najid nodded. Those were his orders to the men he'd left at the roadblocks — kill anyone attempting to enter the village. "Did any escape?"

"No."

Najid pointed toward where the ambush had taken place. To his driver he motioned, "Let's go."

All four men got into the Land Rover and drove up to where the other vehicles were parked. Najid got out. All the men watched him, waiting for his commands. He walked over to the edge of the dirt road and looked at seven people laying face down, each with at least one bullet hole in his body — mostly to the head, some in the back.

Najid looked around. The doctors appeared to have lain down, expecting perhaps to be robbed, not executed.

He turned and looked through a window into the back of the first vehicle. Boxes of medical supplies and some cases with scraped paint and worn edges were stacked. Those medical supplies could have come in handy for the sick townsfolk, but the arrival of the doctors occurred earlier than Najid had hoped. That pushed up Najid's timeline. The townsfolk had fulfilled their purpose of infecting his young, western jihadists. Now, the townsfolk were expendable.

To the men in the HAZMAT suits, he pointed at the doctors' vehicles and said, "Take them to the village." To the men on the roadblock, he pointed at the bodies and said, "Drag them into the jungle. Stay ready. Others will come."

Najid walked up to the man in charge of the roadblock. "Did any of them have radios or telephones?"

"Yes," the man answered.

"Did they call for help?"

"I don't think so," replied the man.

"Where are the devices?"

The man pointed to a spot on the road near the rear of the first vehicle. "Smashed."

Najid looked over toward the broken pieces of electronics scattered in the dirt. "Good."

Chapter 47

The gunshots startled Salim. He looked across the sick and the dying on the floor of the ward. Jalal was looking back at him, frozen. He'd heard the shots, too. Salim slowly looked down at his water pail and cup as if to say, "What do I do with this when we get attacked?"

Jalal shrugged.

Salim heard some shouting outside and the sound of a car speeding off. He looked back down at his pail. It wasn't empty, not nearly. He motioned to Jalal—it was time for an early refill. He stepped over a woman whose eyes were rolling back as she seemed to go into seizures—gurgling, choking on something in her throat. Salim glanced over toward the Tyvek-covered man tending to the boy. He had to be a doctor or a nurse, but he didn't even look up. Salim looked down at the woman. She was just another one dying.

With a shame in his heart that would surely disappoint his instructors from the past few months, he glanced back at the woman as he slowly headed for the door, seriously wondering if he'd died and gone to hell.

Jalal was out the door first and already going down the stairs when Salim let the door slam shut as he hurried down to walk beside him. "What do you think?"

"How many shots did you hear?"

Salim wasn't counting. "Five? Ten? I don't know."

"Did it sound like a gun battle to you?"

Salim shook his head. "No. I didn't hear any automatic weapons. Single shots, mostly."

"Mostly," Jalal agreed.

When they got to the communal well a hundred meters

down the road from the hospital, Salim hung his pail on the hook under the pump and went to work slowly raising the handle, then slowly pushing back down. He watched the stream of cool water fall into the pail. Anything to keep his mind off the horrifically dying and their blood-red, lifeless, zombie eyes.

"Jalal, I can't keep doing this."

Jalal looked down the road and squinted, as though he might be able to divine some information from the cane field, far down where the road curved. "They won't keep us here much longer, I think."

"Why do you say that?" asked Salim, wiping sweat from his brow.

"They don't want us to catch what is killing these people."

"What if we already have it?" It was the first time Salim had that thought, and it frightened him.

"If we were in danger of contracting the disease, we wouldn't be here." Jalal nodded up and down the road. "Look how many of us are in the village. Why would they bring us in and train us, just to catch a disease and die while we're trying to create a cover before going back to the states?"

Salim stopped pumping and looked around at what he could see of the village. "How many of us do you think are here?"

"I'd say a hundred," replied Jalal.

"A hundred? Do you really think that many?"

"I don't know. There are a lot of us."

Salim pulled his pail down and Jalal hung his on the hook, taking his place at the pump.

Jalal, it turned out, had a talent for appearing to be

working hard on the pump while delivering almost no water to the bucket. Salim silently thanked him for his theatrics and took the time to rest and let his mind drift off to oblivion. He didn't want to think about anything. He didn't want to see or smell or touch anything else. He just wanted to leave.

A Land Rover—one of the two dusty new ones that had been parked by the hospital—came speeding up the dirt road.

Salim observed, "Either that was quick, or we've been out here a long time."

"Who cares?" Jalal took his pail off the hook, and the two started their slow walk back toward the hospital building.

The driver of the Land Rover got out, hurrying with weapon in hand into the hospital.

When Salim and Jalal had crossed half the distance to the steps, the HAZMAT guy with the AK-47 came out with the tidy kid's attendant. They stopped on the porch and started talking.

Jalal hesitated. "Slow down. Let them talk."

Salim pointed to the old hospital building off to the left of the new one. "Let's do that one next."

Jalal answered by altering his course a little to the left. However, when they were within a car's length of the new hospital's front porch, one of the men on the porch commanded, "You, there."

Jalal stopped in his tracks. Salim turned and saw the HAZMAT men looking at them. One was pointing at him— it was the one who had heard Austin say the name, Sam.

Chapter 48

The pointing finger skewered Salim's guilty, apostate thoughts, bleeding out their despair. He knew he was caught, and though exposure was tantamount to death, the shame of being caught was wholly consuming. With eyes unable to look at his accuser, he shuffled through the road dust toward the porch stairs with Jalal on his heels.

Salim knew the tidy Arab boy's yellow clad attendant had ratted him out. Nothing had been said at that moment, but at the time there was no man nearby with a gun. But now there he stood on the porch, beside that plastic-covered rooster of a strutting, barking little man.

Salim twitched his face into a tired, innocent guise and went to work on his lie—*the white American kid was delirious*. It was that simple.

Salim repeated the lie in his head. *No!* He'd start with ignorance. The incident was so insignificant that it was hardly worth remembering. Who gave a care about the dying utterances of a delirious boy? What did the boy even say? Salim hadn't even understood him.

Oh, the power of a well-spoken lie, from a face stretched in innocence, the essence of hope.

"Dump those water buckets," said the rooster man, who gestured with a recently acquired AK-47.

Salim looked up and responded by emptying his water into the dirt. Jalal did the same.

The man with the weapon pointed toward the edge of town. "Down there, past that white-walled building, you'll see a rusty tank raised on a metal framework. See if it contains diesel fuel. Let me know how much is inside. Go quickly."

Salim bit his cheek, tasting the warm salt of his own blood. Anything to hide the unexpected joy that comes from sidestepping despair. A grin would have raised a question that he wouldn't be able to answer. He turned on eager feet and took off at his fastest run.

Chapter 49

The nice thing about conference room D-3 was the window, which provided a view of open fields, tall loblolly pines, and sky. Because of the way the building curved back on itself—like an apostrophe with an extra leg—the mirrored glass walls of the cafeteria and another wing of the building were visible.

Rain falling from the overcast sky made Olivia Cooper think about the only thing she didn't like about her job. The NSA's Whitelaw building at Fort Gordon lacked windows. Or that's to say, the windows were there, but they offered views into offices and conference rooms. From the cubes, situated mostly in the center of the building, they couldn't be seen. Days passed—mostly in winter—when she was absorbed in a project, coming in early, having lunch at her desk, and even staying a little bit late, when she wouldn't see the light of day. There was one stretch during the previous winter when she'd worked six consecutive days without seeing the sun. That particular week, they'd worked on Saturday as they had for many Saturdays over those months.

Olivia was excited about the challenge of the new project and the added—though unofficial—responsibility. Her thoughts drifted as the day dragged on. Long hours had a cumulatively deleterious effect on her focus. She needed to jog some long miles. She needed a few good, full nights of sleep. She needed another cup of coffee, and she needed to stop staring out the window at the clouds. Barry was talking to Christine about phone records, and the mention of the name Almasi brought Olivia's thoughts back into the room.

Almasi. Najid Almasi.

The credit card numbers had been tied to an account linked to him. Katherine, the CIA liaison, had nearly sloughed off her mannequin façade and turned into a real, live, excited person when Kevin Sylvan announced the name across the conference room. That was the moment when Olivia's doubts about having wasted the time of overqualified people on a data association game disappeared.

Something real was happening. Something the data would help them sniff out.

Olivia looked at her watch. Eric would be in at any moment. He had a meeting in another wing of the building that had wrapped up ten minutes prior. Before going to the meeting, he promised he'd be right back—Eric was chronically punctual. Minutes later, the conference room door swung open and Eric entered.

He glanced around the room. "Looks like everybody just opened a Christmas present. Olivia, what'd I miss?"

All eyes turned to Olivia.

She drew a quick, calming breath and said, "The accounts have all been tied to Najid Almasi."

Eric was surprised into silence. He looked around the room at confirming nods. "All right," he said, settling back into the seat he'd occupied on and off since the project had taken over conference room D-3. He smiled slyly.

As Olivia started to say something, she couldn't help but notice Barry and Christine—the two who'd been talking about Almasi just a moment before—were squirming in their chairs. To Barry, Olivia said, "You guys came up with something new just before Eric got here?"

"Yes," Barry nodded, then looked over at Christine. "It's good, but it'll be more significant to talk about after you cover the account information."

Olivia motioned toward the screen, "Kevin, would you mind going over the account data for Eric?"

"Sure," he answered, as he stood up and commandeered the cord to the projector. Looking at Eric, he expounded, "I put together a flow chart." Adept with the projector, Kevin got it plugged in quickly, hit a few keys, and seconds later the pull-down screen glowed with a six-foot image of his computer's LCD. "We'll go through this from a bird's-eye view and drill down as necessary into the details."

Kevin stood up and walked over to the wall. It was covered in glowing boxes and triangles connected by labeled lines. He spent ten minutes going through the steps, following the money from the transaction back to an account held by Najid Almasi's father at a Swiss brokerage — an account controlled by Najid. Kevin talked for a moment about how the data had been acquired — at least where that extra information was available — as well as how confident he was with each step in the process. His bet, he explained, was placed on the money coming from Najid Almasi.

"How confident are you?" Eric asked.

Still standing in front of the room with the contents of his computer screen glowing behind him, Eric simply said, "Ninety-eight percent."

"That solid?" Eric was not surprised.

"Yes," Kevin confirmed.

Eric looked around the room. No one voiced disagreement. He stopped on Olivia. "This is your baby. What do you think?"

"I agree with Kevin," she said.

"And you've been over all the data in detail?" Eric

asked.

"In detail. As did Barry and Christine." Olivia tried her best to keep a clinical air about her. Outward excitement over the importance of the account data would undermine her credibility with Eric. It would make him want to look at the data himself.

Eric leaned back in his chair, clasping his hands behind his head. "Good. Very good. I think we can say for certain something is up. Katherine, please notify your boys at the CIA."

"I have," she answered. "Preliminarily. I'll let them know you concur."

"Let's see if we can figure out what we've got here." Eric looked to his right. "Barry—" He stopped and looked back at Olivia.

Olivia was surprised that he was deferring to her. He was trusting her to run the investigation. She swelled with pride as she turned to Barry. "Please tell us what you and Christine came up with."

Barry smiled at Olivia, also deferring, which didn't surprise her. Left to his own devices, Barry Middleton might turn into a brilliant troll living under a bridge, but with someone to lead him who appreciated his talents, Barry was a loyal team player.

He leaned over the table. "This is going to be *really* exciting." All of his pent-up, squirmy excitement was coming through his voice. He took a deep breath and sat back, then looked over to his right. "Christine found it. I'll let her go through the details."

Barry motioned for Kevin to pass the projector connection cable across the table to him. He plugged it into his own computer.

Christine looked away and flushed. She clearly didn't want to be in the spotlight. She cleared her throat, sat up straight in front of her laptop, and pointed at the image of Barry's computer monitor, projecting only blue on the screen. "Barry will have something for us to look at in a second. Without going into the technical details, I was able to collect data that ties a couple of satellite phones to Najid Almasi."

Eric sat up and smiled. "I already like where this is going."

"One of the phones hasn't been used in days," Christine said, "but one has been steadily calling numbers all over Europe and the Middle East for the past forty-eight hours."

"Who is he calling?" Eric asked.

"This is better," Barry interrupted.

The computer screen projected on the wall flashed from solid blue to the image of a map.

Christine proceeded, "I've been focusing on the origin of the calls rather than gathering information about who's on the other end." She pointed at the projected map, and all eyes in the dimly lit room turned to the screen.

Olivia couldn't believe what she was seeing.

Christine continued, "This is a map of eastern Uganda. You know the departure city of each of the airline tickets we're tracking put all of the men in Nairobi. This part of Uganda isn't maybe but a six- or eight-hour drive from there. We think Najid Almasi is in or near a little town in Uganda." She stood up and walked over to the map, pointed to a cluster of short roads at the intersection of two others, north of a big green-colored park area. "Kapchorwa."

Olivia gasped.

Chapter 50

Najid turned away from watching the two young men run. "Seven doctors were coming this way up the road. They are dead now."

Dr. Kassis nodded.

"More doctors will come with soldiers — or without — but there will be more soldiers eventually. We cannot hold out against the Ugandan army if they come in force. We didn't come here prepared for that kind of confrontation."

"So we leave," replied the doctor.

"Yes, we leave. However, we need more time. We need to get these men on their planes before the world understands what evil face this Ebola virus has exposed here. Once they understand that evil — the way that we understand it — we will be out of time." Najid looked down the road at his two runners nearing the place where the diesel tank stood.

"But what do you hope to gain by burning the village?"

Najid turned and looked at Dr. Kassis, unable to read anything unspoken. The Tyvek, the mask, and goggles hid his face. The goggles pulled at the skin on the doctor's face and contorted the subtle movement of muscles around his eyes, and the mask fogged and dripped inside with condensed sweat. Looking at Kassis wasn't much more effective than looking at a telephone for unspoken inflections during a conversation.

Najid took a breath. "I am not an evil man."

"Of course not," Dr. Kassis instantly offered.

"It was never my wish to kill any of these people, certainly not these villagers. They have done nothing, aside from being unlucky enough to be here when airborne Ebola arose." Najid thought for a moment about how to put his thoughts into words. "Perhaps one day if the West prevails, they will work their way back through events and figure out what happened here. If they do, their history writers will paint Najid Almasi in colors more evil than Adolf Hitler. My family's name will become an epithet of evil in the next century."

Najid drew a deep breath to cover the pain he felt at that possibility. Such a thought would be enough to break his father's heart. "But if we prevail, this Kapchorwan incident will be seen as it is, a necessary tragedy. These people, like the soldiers in ten thousand armies since men first picked up swords and swung them at their enemies, unwittingly and unwillingly pay for the victories of their generals and kings."

Najid looked in Dr. Kassis's eyes and did his best to convey the gravity he saw in his decision. "I understand what I do, and why. It is not evil that drives me, but necessity. I wish to keep this strain of Ebola and knowledge of it hidden in this village for as long as I can."

Dr. Kassis said, "Most Africans are uneducated folk."

"I am aware of this." Najid didn't like being schooled, and he let his tone communicate his displeasure.

"You asked for my honesty."

Najid inhaled and tamped his anger. That was an emotion that never led to anything good. "Continue."

"Many of these people do not trust modern medicine. They do not trust doctors or hospitals. You might have seen in your research that in the first two outbreaks of Ebola in 1976—north and west of here in what was Sudan and Zaire at the time—the epicenter of one outbreak was the hospital, and the epicenter *became* the hospital when a few sick Sudanese infected the staff, who in turn infected the other patients."

Najid turned and looked at the hospital doors. "Are you saying that this hospital is the epicenter of this strain of Ebola?"

"I think the whole town of Kapchorwa is, but that is not my point. People talk. Stories spread. The story of fifty villages being devastated by this horrible disease—with Belgian nuns at a hospital being at the source—is a story too wicked not to pass along. I don't doubt that everyone on the continent has heard it. I have little doubt that if these villagers tell scary stories to frighten their children at bedtime, that has got to be one of them."

Najid asked, "What is the point of your story?"

"How many villagers have your men found in their homes?" asked Kassis.

"Many."

"How many more do you think fled the village when they realized what was going on, taking the virus with them? How many do you think ran when we showed up in our yellow suits with guns?"

"Too many," replied Najid.

"My point is that this strain of the virus has traveled outside this village already and is slowly spreading across the country on the feet of frightened peasants."

"I can only hope that the runners are only recently infected, not symptomatic. Some things are beyond my control. I must accept that," said Najid. "It may be a week or two before those turn."

Kassis paused before speaking. "That is an overly optimistic guess."

"That doesn't matter. We are already committed to this course of action. We'll control what we can, and leave the rest to Allah to decide. That will buy us time. Burning the village will not prevent the medical community from figuring out that this strain is airborne, but it will *delay* them finding out. The villagers in the jungle and the men blocking the road will delay them finding out. They will protect that road until they can't. Then they will fade into the forest and shoot any medical personnel they see in the village. All of these things only buy us hours or days. But hours and days are all we need." In Najid's mind, it all made perfect sense.

"But the brutality of burning these people alive!"

"It is a mercy. They'll suffer less in a fire than of the disease. Do you disagree with that?"

"The length of their suffering will be shorter. I can't say that it will be less."

Chapter 51

Everyone in the conference room was staring at Olivia. Olivia was staring at the map. It looked just like the map she'd seen days earlier on Dr. Wheeler's computer.

Eric asked, "Olivia?"

Olivia's heart was racing as she thought of Austin. Could he really be in that tiny Ugandan town with a terrorist? Austin's was probably the only white American face in that town—a town too small for it to go unnoticed. And if he was there in the presence of an Arab, who was executing an operation to terrorize someone or to blow up something, Austin was in the gravest of dangers.

"Olivia?" Eric asked again.

She slowly turned, blinking unexpected tears back into her eyes. She opened her mouth but her voice cracked and gave her away. "My…my brother is there in…in Kapchorwa."

A few jaws dropped. That took them all by as much surprise as it had taken Olivia.

Eric recovered the quickest. "Your brother is in Kapchorwa, Uganda? Right now?"

Olivia nodded.

Eric's confusion showed on his face. He hated coincidences, and everyone knew it. But they also knew they came across them all the time. With enough data and enough time, any two random people or events could be tied together, kind of like that Six Degrees of Kevin Bacon game. "What's he doing in Kapchorwa?"

Olivia looked back at the map and she rubbed her eyes, shaking her head because she didn't believe it herself. "He's there with some kind of college program. He's a senior.

He's volunteering. He's teaching kids." Olivia felt herself falling apart as she thought about her little brother. She always thought of him as little. She'd seen him mostly as a kid, and not as much as a teenager, since she was already off in college or pursuing a career. She'd had a particularly hard time thinking of him as a college student. She shook her head again and turned to hide the tears that were starting to make their way down her cheeks.

Eric turned to Barry and gave him a nod. Barry was now in charge of the project.

Eric stood up and put a hand on Olivia's shoulder. "Come with me. Let's go grab one of the other conference rooms. Let's call—"

"Austin," Olivia said. "His name's Austin."

"Come on."

Olivia stood, fishing for her cell phone in her purse as she did. She couldn't get used to not having it with her.

Eric put a hand on her back and guided her toward the door. "It's okay. I'm sure he's fine. Let's call him from another room.

Eric guided Olivia into one of the small conference rooms. They sat down and Olivia dialed Austin's number. It took an uncomfortably long time for the phone to work its way through the connections. It rang a few times and cut over to voicemail. She looked at the phone and shakily dialed again. Eric patiently watched. She put the phone back to her ear, waited, let it ring, and got voicemail again.

Shaking her head, she placed the phone back in its cradle and looked at Eric. "Voicemail."

"That's okay. It's okay." He put a hand across hers. "Listen to me. I know you're fearing the worst. But the worst almost never happens. You hear me?"

She nodded, knowing Eric's argument was lacking but she had nothing to say about it. "What do I do?"

"Just be calm, Olivia, okay?"

Olivia took a few deep breaths. "It's my brother."

"We don't know anything yet, right?"

Olivia nodded. "I know."

"Okay. I understand why you're worried. I'd be worried too if my brother wasn't such a dipshit."

Olivia laughed through her stress and nodded again. "I love him."

"I know. He's your brother. You have a right to be worried. When was the last time you talked to him?"

Olivia looked down, and a tear rolled over her cheek. "Before he left for Uganda." She started to cry.

Eric leaned over and hugged her.

After a few long minutes, Olivia sniffled up the last of her tears and sat up straight.

"It's okay to cry," Eric told her.

She nodded and gave him half a smile.

"Have you talked to him through email or Facebook? Anything like that?"

"Yes," Olivia nodded. "Of course. Maybe a week ago, he sent me some pictures."

"Has anyone talked to him in the last few days?"

"Maybe my dad," Olivia answered.

"Your dad? Can we call him?"

Olivia picked up the phone and dialed her father's number.

On the third ring, Paul Cooper answered, "Hello?"

"Dad, this is Olivia."

"Is something wrong?"

Olivia started to cry again.

"What's wrong?" Paul asked.

Eric gestured for Olivia to give him the phone. Calmly, he said, "Mr. Cooper, this is Eric Murchison. I'm Olivia's supervisor."

"What's wrong?" Paul asked. "Is Olivia okay?"

"It's okay, Mr. Cooper. Olivia is fine. Everything is all right here."

"It's not all right," Paul said, getting impatient. "She's crying."

"Yes, listen." Eric spoke slowly and calmly, "You know where Olivia works, so you'll understand there's a limit to what I can and can't say. But I'll tell you as much as I can, okay?"

"Alright."

"Olivia is worried about your son, Austin."

"Austin? Why, what happened?" Paul was clearly concerned.

"Nothing that we know of, Mr. Cooper." Eric paused. "As far as we know, there isn't anything at all wrong." He paused again, thinking about what he was going to say next. "Olivia says that your son is in eastern Uganda this summer, teaching kids, is that right?"

"Yes," Paul answered. "That's right. He's in Kapchorwa."

"We're investigating some events in eastern Uganda, and the name of that city came up. Olivia grew very concerned. That's why we called you." Eric nodded at Olivia and smiled reassuringly. "When was the last time you talked to your son?"

"Several days ago. Does this have to do with that Ebola epidemic?"

Eric hesitated before continuing. "We tried to call him, and we can't get through."

"No," Paul replied, "there's no service in Kapchorwa."

"How do you get hold of him when you need to?" Eric asked.

A long pause followed. "I don't know," Paul admitted. "Heidi, my wife, has been trying to get through to him. She's been worried. Tell me, Mr. Murchison, was she right to worry?"

Chapter 52

On the outside of the Tyvek suit, in a pocket Najid had constructed from tape and a piece of plastic, his satellite phone started vibrating. Few people had that number. One of them was his father, who was too far gone to use a phone without assistance. One was Dr. Kassis. Rashid was another. The last was Firas Hakimi. Najid knew what the call was about.

"Speak," Najid said, raising the phone to his facemask.

"You know who this is, I trust." It was the voice of Hakimi.

"I do," answered, Najid.

Hakimi said, "Then you know that I am calling because your friend in Lahore chose to tell me about your bribes before he left this life."

"That is unfortunate. Killing him was not necessary." Najid was disdainful over Hakimi's perpetual inability to face any situation pragmatically. Passion and extremism were the only things that Hakimi understood.

"It will also be unfortunate for you, Najid. Did you expect that you could just buy a hundred and eleven fighters with Western passports and that it would go unnoticed?"

"I did not."

Hakimi didn't like that answer and let his silence grow ominous before saying, "You have been a generous supporter and a friend. Explain to me what you have done, before I decide your fate."

Najid resisted the urge to tell the upstart leader of the movement that he was nothing more than a charismatic puppet, and instead replied, "The questions you ask cannot be answered on a telephone. I will send an emissary to meet your man at the usual place. He will have words for only your ears. Please listen to him before you decide what to do with me. Afterward, I assure you, I will be at your disposal."

"And if I wish to hear these words from your lips?" Hakimi was not happy.

"You cannot get to where I am before the time comes for me to leave. I can only tell you that what I do, I do to further our common cause."

"You are dangerously ambitious for a man who should be kneeling to serve."

Najid knew his father's wealth strengthened his position and made kneeling to Hakimi unnecessary. "The details and depth of my service will become clear when you have spoken to my emissary. He will bring with him the time and place where we can meet and come to an understanding. I assure you, you will not be displeased when you know what I have done."

"It is not for you to decide unilaterally what our brotherhood will do operationally," scolded Hakimi.

"All I can say is that an opportunity arose that required decisive choices and swift action. There was no time to go through our usual process. If what I have done displeases you, I will kneel and accept punishment for my transgressions."

"When can I expect this emissary?" Hakimi asked.

"He will meet your man tomorrow at noon," replied Najid.

"See that he is not late." Hakimi ended the call.

Najid put his soon-to-be-disposed-of phone back in his plastic, makeshift pocket. He looked down the dirt road and spotted one of his recruits hurrying by. "You."

Jalal stopped and looked up. "Yes."

"Come here."

Jalal hurried over and stood in the dirt at the bottom of the hospital steps.

"Where are you from?" Najid asked.

Jalal shuffled nervously.

In a soothing voice, Najid asked, "Tell me where you are from."

"London, sir."

Najid eyed the recruit. "Do you have faith in Allah and our cause?"

"Of course."

"Can you be trusted?"

"I swear to you that I am the most trustworthy of your men," answered Jalal.

"Do you know the name, Firas Hakimi?"

Jalal nervously answered, "Yes. Everyone knows that name."

"I have a message that I will tell you. You will deliver this message personally to him and only to him. Do you know what he looks like?"

"I have seen pictures." Jalal puffed up with pride, "I would be honored to do this."

"Come up here, and listen to me, then."

Najid started constructing his lie.

Chapter 53

Of course he was bright. The CIA wouldn't have had such a hard-on for him if he hadn't been. He was tall. He was good looking. He was athletic. Exactly the kind of guy they'd pick to play James Bond in the movies when Daniel Craig got too old.

But Mitch Peterson never even thought about acting. Instead, he'd spent most of his twenties enamored with his gig as a real spy. Over time his love of his job slowly turned to disappointment and acceptance as he bounced from one do-nothing post to another, in one backwater country after another.

Kampala? None of his buddies from Stanford—now making six and seven figures a year—could even find it on a map.

So he sat in his second-floor office in a building that looked way too much like a high school, gazing out over the embassy wall, watching the sun slowly fall toward the horizon. The trip down the CIA ladder of un-success had a long way to go, and was going too slowly. He checked his watch.

Why did Langley have to set up a time for a call? Why not just call? Why make him wait in his office, pretending to fulfill the duties of a Cultural Attaché, until five-thirty p.m. local time? Mitch fantasized about a microfilm message hidden in a coconut at a dead drop, or a few cryptic words recorded to audio tape that would disappear in a puff of smoke after being heard.

Mitch sighed.

The reality of encrypted phone calls and encrypted emails was so mundane.

He wanted to get out of the office, go for a run, get cleaned up, and go to dinner with his buddy Lou — the son of a Ugandan politician — and hit that new club Lou kept talking about. That was all the excitement his CIA gig in Kampala allowed for, complete with the risk of catching something from the local party girls in a country rampant with HIV.

Sure, he'd gone afield from time to time, chasing down some false alarm about an Al Qaeda something-or-other. The alarms were rare and always led to nothing but a day or two of driving on dusty roads in humid air thick enough to swim in.

When the telephone rang forty-five minutes early, he smiled, thinking it was Langley, early for a nice change. "Peterson, speaking."

"This is Art, can I come in?"

Art McConnell, who was technically his assistant, sat at a desk outside his office, basically fulfilling all the duties of the Cultural Attaché except those where the Attaché's physical presence was required.

"Sure, come in. I'm bored to tears waiting on my five-thirty call."

The phone clicked.

Mitch laid his phone in its cradle and watched Art let himself in. "What's up?"

A haggard Art McConnell crossed the office and sat down in one of the two chairs in front of Mitch's desk. "I need you to talk to this woman I've got on hold."

"What about?"

"Her kid is in some little town up north of Mbale, and she can't get hold of him."

"Jeez, Art. I don't handle that stuff unless the kid is

injured or dead. He's not, is he?"

Art shook his head. "I'm sorry about this, but this woman is relentless. I've been on three calls with her for the better portion of the past three hours."

"Where's she calling from?"

"Denver, Colorado."

Mitch looked at his watch. "Three hours? What is Denver, something like nine hours behind us?"

"Yes, I checked."

Mitch leaned back and threw his feet up on his desk. "So she must be an early riser."

"Yeah, and she probably already drank a pot of coffee because she talks a mile a minute."

Mitch laughed. "That's why you handle this kind of stuff."

Art shook his head. "I can't handle this one, Mitch. She's demanding to talk with you."

"Me, personally?"

"She asked for you by name."

"You told her *my name*?" Mitch got a little angry.

"It's public record, Mitch. She dug around and found your name. I think she dug up information on half the staff. She certainly talked to enough of them."

"Why?"

Art shrugged. "I guess she didn't know who to contact initially, and she got bounced around a bit before she landed on me."

"Why us?"

"The kid is a college student in some kind of volunteer program through a university."

"So we've got a record of the kid, right?" Mitch put his

feet on the floor and rolled closer toward the desk.

"Of course," replied Art.

"And you called the contact with the group?"

"Yes. But he's in Kapchorwa. You know how it is out in the rural parts of the country. I can't get through. The power is probably out or something."

"So tell her to call back." There. Problem solved. That's why Mitch got to sit in the boss's chair, with an office that had an actual door, and a window with a view over boring rooftops.

"I did."

Mitch slumped. "I guess that wasn't successful, or you wouldn't be sitting in here now." Mitch turned toward his computer.

"I told you, she's relentless. She's not going to stop nagging until she talks to somebody with an important-sounding title. I honestly think that if I have to get back on the phone with her, I might start jamming pencils into my eye."

Mitch hung his head and sighed again. He hated talking to families of kids who weren't responsible enough to call or send an occasional email. Sometimes he felt like a babysitter — just a damn babysitter. "*Sharp* pencils?"

"The sharper the better."

"Okay. Summarize for me."

"The kid's name is Austin Cooper. Twenty years old. Between his junior and senior year at Texas A&M."

"Texas A&M. Who goes there?"

Art rolled his eyes. "Don't say that to her. As a matter of fact, don't say anything to her about Texas A&M. You'll get an earful of shit you don't want to listen to. Trust me on that one."

"Got it. No Texas A&M." But Mitch was curious. "What kind of shit?"

"Did you know that Bevo, the University of Texas mascot, supposedly got his name after the Texas Aggies snuck in and branded a football score of 13-0 on his hide?"

"What?" Mitch shook his head. "I don't even know what you're talking about."

"According to her, the UT guys added on to the 13-0 so that it became the word *Bevo*. That's the name of some cow that's their mascot," continued Art. "And that the Aggies allegedly barbequed Bevo and served him at some alumni or football dinner."

"And this woman told you that?"

"Yes," Art smiled. "But I Googled it while she was yammering. It's only about half true."

Mitch frowned and shook his head. "Why'd she tell you this trivial shit again?"

Art shrugged. "I think she knew I had sharp pencils in my desk, and I hadn't shoved one in my eye yet."

They both laughed.

"Mitch, I swear to God, this woman should work for the CIA, interrogating prisoners or something. She'll wear 'em down with her pointless bullshit."

"Great." Mitch thought *he* should be doing that for the CIA. Well, not really, but it was better than talking to lonesome mothers from Denver whose sons were trying desperately to hack off the apron strings. "So this woman's from Denver. What's her name?"

"Heidi Cooper."

"And the kid. You said, Austin, right? Austin, really? Who names their kid after a city?"

"Apparently, a dad who's completely nuts about his

alma mater." Art shook his head, reached out with a piece of paper, and laid it on the desk in front of Mitch. "Those are the particulars. The bottom line is, she's worried about the kid, can't get hold of him, saw something on the Internet about Ebola road blocks in Uganda, and she wants us to do something."

"Like what?"

"Aside from finding the kid and telling her he's all right, I don't know," answered Art.

"She didn't tell you?"

"I couldn't hear that part. I had a pencil stuck in my eye."

Mitch grinned. "Does it affect your hearing?"

"Depends on how far you push it in."

Mitch picked up the paper and scanned down. He looked up at the clock. "It's a quarter to five. You get on the phone, tell her I've been in a meeting with somebody important, but I've got time to talk to her now. Be sure and tell her this next part. Tell her I've got a meeting at five o'clock I can't be late for. And Art, if I'm still on the phone with her at five, you come into my office and rescue me. Got it?"

"Got it."

"Okay. Put her through."

Chapter 54

"Yes, yes. I understand." Mitch looked at the clock. Five twenty-eight. He'd been trying to get off the phone since five o'clock. Art was right about wanting to stick a pencil in his eye. "Listen, Mrs. Cooper—Mrs. Cooper." Stopping the stream of words was like stepping in front of a train. "Mrs. Cooper!"

She paused for a breath.

"Please, listen for just a moment." Mitch risked a breath, hoping she wouldn't start up again in that tiny moment, "We'll do everything we can to check up on Austin. I promise you. I have a call starting in two minutes, and there is no way I can miss it. Does Art have your number?"

"Yes, but you really—"

"Mrs. Cooper, please. We have your number. I'll call. I've really got to go. It was good speaking with you." Mitch hung up the phone. He yelled, "Art!"

Art hurried through the door with a question on his face.

"Ugh!"

Art smiled. "Should I sharpen some pencils for you?"

"Good God. If she calls back, please handle it."

"I'll try."

Mitch groaned. "Please *do* try. And try to find that kid of hers before she calls back."

"I'm working on it."

Mitch looked at his watch. "I've got to get on this call. Close the door, please."

Art smiled, nodded, and quietly pulled the door shut as he stepped out.

Mitch picked up his secure phone, navigated the

procedure for establishing a secure connection, and found out he was the first one on the call. He breathed a sigh and leaned back in his chair, wondering what the call was about. Before his imagination went too far adrift, the line clicked.

"Hello?" Mitch asked.

"Hello," replied his boss, back in Langley — or wherever Jerry Hamilton was. "It's just us on the call."

"What's up?"

Jerry said, "We've picked up some information concerning a Najid Almasi. He associates with some naughty Arab boys that like to posture and blow things up."

"Which ones?" Mitch asked.

"Doesn't matter," said Jerry. "He's been in and out of the fringes of whatever group is in the headlines for the past decade."

"Almasi. The name is familiar," said Mitch.

"His father is in the oil business. Shitloads of money. The name comes up from time to time, but we haven't established a firm link, so you may have seen it in a report somewhere. The old man is dying. He's been dying for a couple of years now. Some kind of cancer, and the son — Najid — has been taking over control of the family business. I've sent over the details in a secure file."

"Gotcha." Mitch logged into his computer.

"We think Najid has ambitions. He's some kind of jihadist up-and-comer."

Mitch smiled, thinking of what tended to happen to guys who rose to the top of those org charts. "Big dreams."

"Yes. We've picked up some information concerning Najid that we're trying to piece together. He's shifting money out of stocks and into hard assets. He's shorting airline stocks—"

"Airline stocks?" That sort of activity always raised the curiosity of intelligence types.

"He's gone long on pharma companies, weapons manufacturers, and other crazy shit, all on margin. He bought all the bullets in the warehouse from a Pakistani manufacturer."

"Their stuff is shit, you know that, right?" Mitch said, "He doesn't have high standards."

"It's about logistics, not quality."

Mitch got lost, which wasn't common. "Logistics? What do you mean?"

"He's having them shipped to the family compound on the Red Sea, paying a premium to get them there in a hurry."

"What else?" Mitch asked.

"Food."

"What do you mean?"

Jerry said, "He bribed the crew of an aid ship to Somalia, or some such place, and diverted it to the same place the bullets are going."

Mitch thought about that for a moment. "He converted his assets, then placed his bets on long and short positions on margin? He starts building up the biggest doomsday hoard at the family compound. Got it. How much money did he bet on his stock plays?"

"Tens of millions on bets that shouldn't have any hope of paying off."

"Something is definitely up. Maybe he's just scared shitless over the Ebola threat," Mitch said.

Jerry moved right on. "We have reason to believe he's in

Uganda now."

"Here?" Mitch sat up straight in his seat. "Where? Do we know?" He didn't expect an exact answer on that, but he got one.

"Some little town near the Kenyan border. Kapchorwa."

Mitch paused. "Kapchorwa? You're kidding me."

Suddenly concerned, Jerry asked, "What do you know about Kapchorwa?"

"Nothing, really," said Mitch. "I just got off the phone with some mother whose son is in Kapchorwa, and she's freaked out about not hearing from him, with all of these Ebola rumors."

"What's the situation with the rumors there? Have there been any confirmed cases in Uganda yet? Or more specifically in the Kapchorwa district?"

Mitch continued. "Nothing official yet, but the rumors have been going around all week about cases in Mbale, which is a couple hours south of Kapchorwa. Some WHO teams have been sent to the area, but there's a bit of an uproar because no one's heard from them. At least one of the doctors is an American, so the Ambassador has been involved in meetings on and off about it all day."

"What's your gut tell you on this one? Is there an Ebola outbreak in eastern Uganda?"

Mitch thought about that for a moment before answering. "With Sudan to the north, and Congo both south and east of us, we're in the general vicinity of historical Ebola outbreaks. So that part isn't out of the question at all. But there's a lot of fear, and of course a ton of disinformation about it. You know there are religious groups here convincing people that faith in God will protect them from Ebola or that Ebola is a hoax?"

"You're kidding me," mumbled Jerry.

"No, real deal. Then there's the social stigma. Nobody wants his peers to shun him because he's tainted with Ebola. There's a lot of reason here to hide it. So taking all of those factors together, it could be here, or it couldn't. The only way to know for sure is to get confirmation from a doctor who has seen it himself. So far, we don't have that."

"Mitch—" That was unusual, they never used one another's names on these calls. "Information has come to us through the ambassador's office that another WHO team is assembling to go to that part of the country. Get yourself included. See if you can convince them to get on the road tonight, if you're able. Fly, if possible. Bring some security if you can. Be discreet, but do it. If this Najid character is up in Kapchorwa, and he thinks there's an Ebola outbreak underway, he's only there for one reason."

"You think he wants to collect samples so he can weaponize it?" Mitch hoped the answer was no. Was it possible that could be done?

"That's the fear."

Mitch asked, "Do these guys have the resources for that kind of work?"

"I doubt it, but you never know, right? We need to find out," Jerry reckoned.

Mitch rubbed his face without even thinking about it, and thought about the right way to say what he was going to say next. "If I find Najid in Kapchorwa, what do you want me to do?"

"Learn what you can. If he's there, you may find out whether he's a shadowy knucklehead who keeps bad company and makes bad choices, or whether he's an aspiring player. If he's a player, he's a well-funded, potentially dangerous enemy."

"I understand."

"Call in the cavalry if you need to. I'm trying to get approval to send a team your way."

"Already?" That surprised Mitch. "You're that serious about this?"

"Don't get too excited. I may not be able to get it approved. I'll send you their information if I get it arranged. Listen, this is a top priority — urgent."

"I understand."

"Keep me in the loop," said Jerry.

"I will." Mitch hung up the phone.

Chapter 55

The Land Rovers and two more vehicles taken from the dead doctors up the road were headed east, loaded with young jihadists. Salim, wondering what had happened to Jalal, was with several dozen others using empty waste buckets and any other container they could find to douse every structure in Kapchorwa with diesel. On that point, the rooster man was explicit. Every structure would burn—the houses, the storage sheds, the pile of bodies behind the hospital, and the buildings housing the sick townsfolk.

It was with a sick stomach that Salim thought about all those dying people. It was with tremendous guilt that he thought about Austin. What was Austin doing in the middle of Africa? Austin, the same guy who'd been so patient in helping him with his Algebra homework when they'd been freshmen at Thunder Ridge High School, even when the rest of their friends teased him for being the only Indian in the world who had difficulty with mathematics. As if every brown-skinned person in the world was from India. They just couldn't accept that his family was from Pakistan.

Simple-minded bigots, with racism wrapped in jokes and topped with smiles. That's what Salim thought of most of those kids.

Nevertheless, through high school Austin and Salim hung around in the same group. They'd gone to movies together with their friends and had dinner at each other's houses. Salim knew Austin's parent's names, his dogs' names, the familiar smell of their house, and Heidi's cooking—especially her homemade ravioli. It was bad enough that his friend was dying of a vicious tropical disease, but Salim was being asked to burn him alive.

Vehicles of every sort started to arrive in the village from the east and were parked at the eastern edge of Kapchorwa.

After the tank of diesel fuel was emptied and spread over the houses, many men, presumably all Westerners like Salim, got into the trucks and headed toward Kenya. Salim was one of a dozen left at the west end of the village. They went to work binding dry grass into bundles, and Salim immediately guessed their purpose—torches.

Salim's commander put him at the southwestern corner of the village, where circular grass-roofed huts fringed the town. They would burn easily. The commander lit one of Salim's bundles and directed him to move along the edge of the town, lighting each house as he went. Still in sight of the other torchbearers, Salim struggled to light the first hut, then walked quickly to the next one in the row. Before lighting the building, he peered inside and thanked Allah it was empty.

He hurried to the next. Also empty.

At the fifth hut, the story changed. A man lay on a blanket where a decrepit woman tended to him. The smell of the disease was overpowering. The man would die. Looking at the woman, Salim guessed she would quickly follow the man down that dark road.

What kind of disease kills everybody?

Salim stood in the door with his torch burning, contemplating that thought. Maybe that's why they were leaving all of a sudden. Maybe the disease was something other than typhoid? Maybe it was something that *killed everybody*. If that was the case, then it was a good thing they were getting out of town before they became infected.

Infected?

Salim laid his palm on his forehead to check for a fever.

There was none. He had no symptoms of any kind. The momentary fear passed.

With all doubt gone about what was going to happen to the two wretches on the floor, Salim couldn't burn the hut with them inside. He couldn't bypass the hut, either. To do that would risk the wrath of his commander—a wrath that would likely be his own death.

He closed his eyes, not believing that he was doing it. In clear view of the woman sitting on the floor, Salim raised his torch and lit the edge of the thatched roof. Her eyes went wide, then dropped. She looked down at her man on the floor. Her evolution through surprise, anger, hate, and despair disturbed Salim in a way he couldn't quite believe. How could people give up so easily?

He let his torch fall to the dirt, ran inside, dropped to a knee beside the man and lifted him, surprised by how light he was. Hoping the woman would follow, he ran through the door, past caring if anyone saw what he was doing. If he was seen, he'd just keep running. He'd figure out how to make his own way back to Denver at some point down the road.

No one was outside to witness his transgression. Salim hurried across a wide dirt path with the woman making every effort to keep up. Even though he was burdened with carrying her stick figure of a husband, the disease was taking a heavy toll on her. He crashed into a field of towering sugar cane, pushing through the stalks, hoping the couple would be well hidden inside. The woman struggled behind him—grunting, wheezing, and pushing against the cane.

When Salim figured he was far enough in, he stopped and looked back. He couldn't see through the tall crop. They were deep enough. The woman fell to her knees and emptied the reddish-black contents of her stomach onto the ground.

"Sorry," Salim told her as he lay the man in the red dirt. "I'm so sorry." Without looking back, he took off at a sprint toward the burning village, already glowing orange in the sky over the field.

Chapter 56

Oily black smoked settled to the ground all through the village. Gray smoke blew over his head. Night grew darker in the sky as the fire grew up to meet it. Salim retrieved his bundles of grass, lit one on the last hut he'd torched, and ran onward. But instead of going on to several small buildings close to the road, he instead took off across an open field, the shortest distance to the hospital.

With the glow of the fire ruining everyone's night vision, he hoped no one would notice his sole lit torch running across the field. Structures were going up in flames through the town from east to west. He wasn't the only one hurrying through the task of burning.

He tripped, got a face full of dirt, and his torch bounced across the rough ground in front of him. Thankfully, the fall didn't extinguish it. A thought crossed his mind that he shouldn't get up. His jihadist brothers were going to be in a hurry to leave the burning township. They'd likely not even notice his absence.

Rising up on his hands and knees and to his feet, he knew the question of whether or not he got on one of those trucks headed east wasn't as important as getting to the hospital's back door before it was set ablaze.

Salim picked up his torch and ran.

As he approached the back of the hospital, he saw he didn't have much time. The other jihadists were past the town's central intersection and were working their way up the road toward him.

Bodies behind the hospital were strewn in piles large and small, with some from earlier cleanups laid next to one another in neat rows. Salim touched his torch to the cloth that wrapped the first body, near its feet. It had diesel fuel on it, and after a little coaxing, it burst into flames that jumped quickly to the adjacent bodies. Those burning bodies were the cornerstones of the hope he needed to make his desperate plan work. None of his comrades would come around to the back of the hospital to light the bodies if they saw them in flames already.

Salim hurried past body after body, lighting as he went. He reached the largest pile, lit it in several places, and stepped back for a few seconds to watch the flames crawl with red fingers across the crumpled cloth that wrapped them. He tossed his torch to the top of the pile and ran to the hospital's back door. A half-dozen bodies were piled outside the door to prevent it from opening. Salim grabbed the feet of the one on top and dragged it out of the way. The second followed. He rolled a few more away and pulled others far enough from the door that he was able to get it open.

It was then that Salim realized he would need to light those bodies, too. If he didn't, anyone coming around to check the backside of the building—not that it would happen, but it could—would see the door unblocked. Burning bodies just outside the door would keep it hidden.

Salim pulled one of the smaller grass bundles from where he had it tucked in his belt, ran to the nearest fire and lit it. He heard voices. The others were getting close.

Running back to the door as the sickly smell of burning flesh mixed with the diesel and smoke, he quickly lit the scattered bodies and flung the door open. The lantern light in the room seemed dim compared to the conflagration outside. He cast a fearful look at the front door and ran to the center of the room. Patients who could were getting up on their hands and knees, panic in their blood-red eyes.

Some fell right back down. Others slept—good for them. Many were too sick to have any awareness of the flaming horror coming their way.

Salim saw immediately that the tidy Arab boy's cot was empty and the yellow HAZMAT doctor was gone. Austin was getting up on shaky knees and looking out a window when Salim arrived at his side. "Can you run?"

Austin looked at him as if he didn't understand.

"Can you—?" *To hell with it.* Salim lifted Austin to his feet, and threw Austin's arm over his shoulder. As Austin tried to stand and struggled to walk, Salim was forced to drag him toward the center aisle.

Austin pulled back and pointed at a box by the tidy boy's cot.

Medical supplies.

Salim managed to grab a cardboard flap on the box then move as fast as he could toward the back door. Ambulatory patients understood fear and urgency, and started to make their way to the door, some shuffling slowly, most of those struggling to stay upright, a few on hands and knees.

"Margaux?"

"What?" Salim asked.

Austin repeated, "Margaux."

The white girl.

Damn.

"I'll try." Salim got Austin and the box through the back door. Austin's feet seemed to become more useful once they were outside, moving quickly past the largest pile of burning bodies. Austin stopped, jerked his arm away from Salim, and stood on his own feet. "Margaux. Help her."

"I can't."

"Please. The others."

Salim slumped. Having succeeded in rescuing Austin—a feat he didn't expect to live through—he deflated. A second rescue would surely fail.

"Take the box. Go to the trees." Salim turned and ran to the back door.

He didn't see any of his brothers coming around the side of the building, but a few of the sick villagers had come out. "Run to the trees!" he commanded as he pushed past another of the patients coming through the back door.

The situation inside the ward was chaos, for as much that can be said about people who could barely muster the energy to take care of the most basic necessities in the bucket next to their beds. Several were trying to get the front door open. Some were staring out of windows. Many were yelling some kind of nonsense.

Mostly, they were just stinking and dying in peaceful comas. The disease had made sure of that.

Back beside Austin's cot, Salim dropped on his knee beside the white girl. She was in terrible shape. Salim had seen enough of the sick to know she was destined to die. He saw her chest rise and fall, so she wasn't dead already. He picked her up, threw her over his shoulder, and started toward the back door. A gush of hot liquid poured over his back as Margaux retched. Salim cursed, knocked another patient aside, and made it to the back door.

He heard the front door bang. The patients trying to get out inadvertently kept the jihadists out front for the last seconds he needed. He pushed through the back door and slammed it closed behind him. Anybody still inside would have to deal with their own fate. Salim knew several buckets of diesel were sitting just inside the front doors, and he knew someone would open those doors, kick the buckets over, and throw in a torch. The diesel, the bedding, and the people would flame up in seconds.

The explosion of shrieks behind him told Salim the fire inside had started. He didn't look back.

Chapter 57

Some things just seem to take forever, and the greater the push to speed them up, the slower they seem to go. Mitch sighed loudly and looked at his watch as he leaned against the open door of the truck. He looked inside at the driver — a Ugandan who shrugged, making it clear that it wasn't his fault. Of course it wasn't. They both knew it.

One hundred and eighty miles from Kampala to Kapchorwa. Getting there had grown into a fiasco of *wait-a-few-minutes* that turned into hour-long delays that eventually burned off the whole morning. It was too late in the evening after Mitch got off the call with his boss to head out the night before. Everyone agreed on that. But the group of doctors heading to the villages north of Mbale — into ground zero of the Ebola rumors — wouldn't go without an armed escort. Apparently two attempts by the WHO to head up the road to those villages left a single doctor unaccounted for, and another group of doctors and aid workers, as well.

Everyone anticipated trouble up that way, though nobody knew how that trouble would manifest itself.

Dripping with sweat in the sun, Mitch stood impatient and bored, glaring at the doctors. Three of them were standing in front of their vehicle that was parked behind his in a makeshift caravan. Another truck, right behind theirs, carried more people along with boxes of medical gear.

One of the doctors kept talking about machete-wielding bandits he'd encountered during a stint in Rwanda. He was certain the road north of Mbale held an ambush of just such men. One of the doctors seemed to think the best way to assuage the other doctors' fears was to talk about how, during the 1976 Ebola outbreak in Zaire, the area around the Ebola river—for which the nasty little Filovirus was named—had turned into a veritable black hole. No word, no communication of any kind came out.

Mitch didn't care if it was the Bermuda Triangle. He had a compact Glock in a holster on his belt, thoroughly hidden by his baggy shirt. The man in the back seat—a guy he'd used for security on more than one occasion—had an AK-47 standing on the floorboard beside him. Two more AK-47s were covered under a blanket on the other side—one for Mitch and one for the driver, who was also experienced at using it. Both carried concealed handguns. Mitch preferred to work with experienced, prepared men.

He also preferred to get things done. So whether their escort from the Uganda People's Defence Force—the army —showed up or not, he was leaving at noon. The sound of a big diesel engine caught his attention and he looked down the street. As the dust cleared, a squad of Ugandan soldiers in a big flatbed truck appeared, only a day late.

Chapter 58

Driving through Kampala near noon left them in more traffic than Mitch had wanted to deal with. At least with the vehicle moving and the windows down, the breeze blowing in felt nearly as cool as if the air conditioner was running. With the elevation, the summer in Kampala wasn't as hot as he'd imagined it would be before he arrived nearly a year ago.

They passed modern buildings and houses, as well as less affluent areas of town, and slums. The highway passed Mandela National Stadium as they were leaving Kampala and stretched into the smaller outlying towns. It occurred to Mitch how much the country reminded him of the rural parts of the Deep South—Alabama or Mississippi, maybe—where he could drive past a brightly colored eight-pump gas station one moment, and in the next, past farm shacks covered in flaking paint with rusting metal you-name-its in the front yard. Where chickens ran loose among barefoot kids who looked like they couldn't care less when their next bath time arrived, and weeds as tall as the kids grew wherever their feet didn't beat them down to bare dirt.

Eventually, the houses and businesses thinned out to farming country, and they drove past tea and cane fields stretched over the plains and up the distant hills—lush greenery growing in yellowish-red dirt. The countryside took on a sameness as they sped along a paved four-lane highway. Houses, farms, trees, hills... repeat.

A few hours into the drive, they stopped at a roadside market. Stacks of crates and tables filled with all manner of fruits and vegetables were displayed under the shade of sheets of painted tin held up on wooden frames. Several farmers' wives ran the little market and collected money from the soldiers and doctors as they meandered through and picked out a few things to eat.

At first Mitch worried about Ebola in the fruit, but his knowledge of how the disease spread was woefully thin. In the end, peer pressure and hunger pushed him to buy a few mangos for the long ride.

After several hours on the road, they reached Mbale. The army truck with its load of bored soldiers worked its way through the slowly moving traffic, with the other vehicles behind. It wasn't until well after four o'clock that the caravan drove north out of Mbale and toward the little collections of farmhouses on the road to Kapchorwa.

Twice along the road, the doctors brought the convoy to a halt at certain clumps of houses and huts so they could get out and talk to residents about their health. When they got out at each stop, the medical workers would put on surgical masks and gloves. Mitch thought it wise to do the same. Those stops dragged on past the point of boredom. Mitch wandered among the houses and bushes, observing the people and looking for anything out of the ordinary. It was clear early on that not one of the farmers was going to admit to anything. Mitch spied several at the first stop taking off across a cornfield. They didn't want anything to do with soldiers or doctors.

Some farmers stood far back inside their houses and talked from there. Others who talked to the doctors outside their huts kept a distance from them and denied that anyone they knew or were related to was sick. Talk of Ebola was everywhere, but the disease itself was always a rumor away in the next tiny village up the road or around the bend.

They found no direct evidence of the disease. But at each stop, Mitch grew more and more certain that it was lurking nearby. He was careful to avoid touching anything or anyone. He didn't drink water at any place they stopped. Although he was growing hungry with the dinner hour upon them, he made no more purchases from roadside markets.

They passed the military roadblock, and what they learned from the men there was no different than anything else they'd heard or seen on their trip: rumors and worry.

With the army roadblock twenty or thirty minutes behind them, it was starting to get dark. Mt. Elgon's peak and higher elevations glowed orange and red in the light of the setting sun. Male cicadas started their distinctive nighttime song, and nocturnal birds added their calls.

Mitch was staring at the colors slowly changing on the mountainside, not paying any attention to what was going on around him, when the driver slowed the vehicle in response to the squeaking brakes of the military truck up ahead. The road was dirt by then—they'd been off pavement since a few miles out of Mbale—and a cloud of red grit surrounded them.

Mitch coughed and blinked the dust away as he disembarked from the truck, not really curious about why they stopped. It was more out of boredom as he looked for something to do.

The doctors in the vehicle ahead—they were all doctors to Mitch—were all out by then, with a few walking forward, perhaps to relieve their own boredom. Mitch passed by one of the doctors standing by the vehicle, "What's up?"

"Don't know." The guy answered. "I was asleep."

The road dust was settling, more than a little of it in Mitch's hair and on his clothes. He walked up to two doctors at the rear of the army truck—one man, one woman

—who were looking at a few felled trees blocking the road ahead. The soldiers were standing by the trees, looking around, gesturing, and assessing the situation. They knew they'd be tasked with clearing the road and were talking it through.

"We're here," the female doctor said.

The man—soft, young, pale-skinned, and maybe not even old enough to be a doctor—asked the woman in a high school kid's voice, "Why do you say that?"

She pointed at the trees down in the road. "Villagers do this when they want to isolate themselves from sickness, to keep it out."

A single shot cracked through the air, and the soft young man crumpled.

Before Mitch could react, more shots followed. The air was full of whizzing bullets and the sound of automatic weapons fire. He dove behind the truck, dragging the woman down with him into the dirt. Mitch was on his knee behind a big rubber wheel with his compact Glock instinctively in his outstretched hand, looking for targets that would be way too far away to hit.

The soldiers ran back from the downed trees and around behind the truck. A few jumped up inside and retrieved their weapons, passing them quickly down to the others.

The gunfire still came. Mitch couldn't find a target.

The UPDF soldiers—armed and as organized as they were going to be—took a defensive position behind the truck, while leaning over and spraying off shots down the road.

The female doctor cried out and Mitch realized she wasn't behind the cover of the truck. She had gone over to help the downed man. Mitch lowered his pistol and holstered it. He leapt across the open ground between the truck and the man, grabbed a handful of the wounded man's shirt, and dragged him behind the truck. The woman voiced her gratitude, but by then Mitch was looking around, feeling vulnerable to an ambush from either side.

The doctor began working fervently on her downed coworker as he struggled to breathe, bleeding profusely from a bullet hole in his chest.

Mitch caught the attention of a few of the soldiers and pointed to the trees and bushes on both sides of the road behind them. They caught his meaning right away. Mitch knelt down beside the doctor. "Can he be moved?"

"He needs a hospital," she shouted above the gunfire.

Without much thought about his own safety, Mitch shoved his arms beneath her patient and hoisted him up with a grunt. "C'mon." He charged as fast as he could move with the extra weight of the incapacitated man.

Mitch lifted him inside the back door of the doctors' truck. His two escorts were immediately beside him with weapons at the ready. Turning to address the woman, he shouted, "Follow us. We'll escort you back to Mbale. I know where the hospital is there." He ran back to his truck and jumped into the driver's seat.

His two men didn't need to be told what to do. They each took a seat inside and trained their weapons out a window on either side. Moments later, they were racing back down the road to Mbale, with the medical people following as closely behind as speed and the dust allowed.

Chapter 59

It had been a rough ride. After leaving Kapchorwa in the back of a farm truck with guys who were dirty, sweaty, and blackened with ash, they watched Kapchorwa's flames grow in the night sky. Over the course of enough miles, the flames turned to a western glow in the darkness. There was only the rumble of the engine, the rattle of the old truck, and the grunts of the unnamed jihadists in the back with Salim. Each time the tires rolled through a particularly big hole in the road, they'd all bounce off the truck's bed. Salim earned a new bruise with each landing.

The sky slowly opened up to black and a billion pinpricks of stars, most of which Salim had never seen. Denver cast off too much light pollution for much of anything to be visible in the night sky. The truck left the road after driving for maybe an hour, earning Salim and his compatriots plenty more bruises. The truck moved much too fast for safety—much less comfort—across rough ground. Throughout what seemed like an unending trip, none of them spoke. Mostly they stared with the empty looks of men who'd done something that shamed their souls. To fight America's tyrannical, selfish policies by shooting at soldiers in the field was one thing, but burning sick people in their homes was another altogether.

Somewhere in the chaos of preparing for the burning, Jalal had disappeared. Whether burned in the village, beheaded for disobeying, or on another truck headed east, Salim could only guess. To take his mind off of the atrocities in the village, he spent a lot of time guessing what might have happened to Jalal and imagining about how they might meet up again. At the moment, Jalal was the only real friend he had. Well, perhaps Austin was a friend. He'd risked his life to save Austin and the girl with the weird French name he couldn't remember.

Eventually the truck arrived at another dust-covered road. The ride became smoother, and the truck moved faster. The tallest tip of Mt. Elgon started to glow pink in the early sun. They had to be east of the mountain then, back in Kenya, and morning was coming.

Salim watched the mountain change as washes of morning color crept down the slopes. He thought of lava pouring out of the extinct volcano. The country on both sides of the road emerged from blackness, and Salim saw farm after farm after farm growing all manner of crops he couldn't identify. In many ways, it reminded him of eastern Colorado with its rolling hills and plains covered with farms, pastures, and majestic mountains rising in the west.

It wasn't until he was shaken awake that he realized exhaustion had gotten the better of him, and he'd dozed off.

"Wake up, brother. You can sleep on the plane."

"The plane?" Salim asked, realizing the truck's engine was off. The truck was empty, and he could see his companions walking toward a dilapidated building.

The Arab man pointed in the direction of the other men. "Follow them. You can wash off when you get inside. You'll get new clothes."

"The plane?" Salim asked, realizing only then that his bag, his passport, and his billfold were gone.

The man guessed the question. "Your things are inside."

Salim slowly stood, feeling the physical abuse he'd put himself through over the past days.

"Hurry. Your plane leaves in thirty minutes."

"Okay," Salim jumped down off the bed of the truck, wobbled on his knees, and followed the others toward the shabby building.

Looking around in the dawn, it occurred to him that he hadn't slept that long. Mt. Elgon still stood tall off toward the west. The surrounding land was mostly flat farmland with the exception of the rural airport and a few cobbled-together municipal buildings. A runway stretched off in two directions. A commuter plane sat on the tarmac, looking large enough to hold everyone in the truck and maybe a few more.

Besides the building the men were being herded toward, only one other small building, with an array of oddly-shaped antennae on the roof, stood on the immediate property. A curved wall of square window panes faced the runway. It had to be the terminal.

Perhaps this was the first real step on the way home to Denver.

Once inside the building, Salim guessed it had to be a hanger, built to house two or three small private planes, which were absent. At one end, the other men from the truck were either naked and washing themselves with soap and a garden hose, or stripping and waiting their turn.

Salim took his place in line, waiting as men hurried through their cleaning in front of him. Toward the far end of the hangar, a few tables with pants and shirts in various colors in Western styles lay on the table. On the floor leaning against a wall he spied his travel bag.

It was the first thing he had to feel good about in days.

Exactly thirty minutes after Salim rolled himself out of the bed of the truck, the commuter plane taxied down the runway and climbed into the thin Kenyan air. Some in the passenger cabin seemed to know each other and hushed conversations ensued. Salim contented himself to watch the houses and trees below shrink and merge into colored patterns with the other features on the ground.

A man came up out of the rear of the plane, passing out bottles of water and food.

Another man stood up at the front of the plane with a satchel he then handed to a guy on the first row. "Inside is an envelope with your name on it. Find your envelope and pass the bag to the next man. We will be landing in Nairobi in forty minutes. Some of you have flights leaving shortly after we arrive. You'll find airline tickets and itineraries in your envelope with your information. You will also find credit cards in your name and cash in the currency of your country of origin. All of you have connecting flights and long layovers. You'll each be traveling for most of the next two days."

The plane bounced through some turbulence and the speaker fell to the side, hitting roughly against the door. When he stood back up, embarrassed, he shrugged and smiled. A few of Salim's compatriots chuckled softly. It was almost normal.

The speaker straightened himself out and put his serious face back on. "While you are in each airport, walk around, learn what you can about the security, the layout, and look for weaknesses. Don't write anything down that could be used as evidence to detain you. You each have a prepaid cell phone in your envelope. A phone number has been added to the contact list for someone called Mother. Mother will call you to give you instructions. If you need to call for questions, call Mother, but don't make a habit of it. We know what your schedules are, so don't worry if you find yourself coming to the end of your itinerary. We'll contact you with instructions before that."

More turbulence but the speaker caught himself on a seat back and smiled confidently. "Otherwise, enjoy your

Western lives. Eat at restaurants. Spend the money. Smile, just like holiday travelers. Talk with other passengers, get to know them. The hard part is behind you. From here forward, your main purpose is to fit back into the country you came from. Don't spend any time worrying about when you will be called up for a mission. That day is far in the future."

Chapter 60

Mitch spent the evening and the night in the hospital. His first impulse was to leave the doctors and aid workers there with their wounded man, pull some strings to get the Uganda People's Defence Force in gear, and go back to the village that night. The more he thought about it, the more he came to believe whatever was going on up the road had to do with the Ebola outbreak. And as much as his intuition told him Ebola and terrorism were intersecting up that road, it was his task to find proof of that. He was a disgruntled, self-proclaimed embassy playboy, out to do his part in the War on Terror. The agency must have been taken by surprise to dump all of this in his lap.

With his options waning, he stayed in the hospital and befriended the woman who'd been near him when her coworker was shot. The woman, a Dr. Mills from Tampa, Florida, was young, dark-haired, and athletic—exactly the kind of girl he'd try to bed. But that wasn't why he'd cozied up to her. If terrorists were up that road to Kapchorwa fiddling with a way to weaponize Ebola, he'd need help from at least one doctor in putting those pieces together.

The wounded guy died sometime around three a.m., putting the doctors into a frenzy of heated arguments and phone calls. Mitch—by then on a first-name basis with the survivors—stayed on the fringes and nudged them to go back. He tried convincing them that they needed to find out what was *so* important up that road that it needed to be protected.

In the end, he won. Not completely, but enough. Dr. Mills and another doctor named Simmons agreed to go back with Mitch, provided the army went first and secured the village. On that particular point, Mitch had been assured by his boss that the UPDF was heading up that road in force at sunup.

So after sleeping too few hours, and eating something from a food vendor on the street, Mitch loaded his two doctors into a truck, along with his two men from the day before, and four more armed contractors in another vehicle which took the lead.

Six menacing, quiet black men with guns made the doctors feel more secure. Knowing the army had gone ahead several hours earlier helped a lot with that feeling.

Chapter 61

When they finally drove into Kapchorwa, Dr. Mills quietly shuddered, "My God."

Everyone else in the truck was silent as they drove around an armored vehicle parked in the road with a man standing up through a hole in its roof behind a machine gun. Soldiers were milling around or searching through the remains of burned houses.

At the intersection of two dirt roads that was the center of the tiny town, three military vehicles were parked. Four men who appeared to be the officers in charge stood engaged in discussion. Mitch had the driver stop the car near them. He got out with Dr. Mills in tow, skillfully handling the introductions, making it clear that he was the American Cultural Attaché from Kampala, here to find a missing American college student, and that the doctors were present to search for signs of an Ebola outbreak.

Mitch then asked what had happened. The soldiers had only secured the town a half hour earlier, killing nine Arab gunmen in the process. Aside from the obvious — that the place had been systematically burned — no one knew what had transpired or why.

With a clear warning to Mitch and the doctors that the army couldn't be responsible for their safety, the army officers went back to their business.

Mitch turned toward Dr. Mills, seeing past her that his hired gunmen were out of the cars, casually holding their weapons, ready for whatever might come. Mitch looked around at the blackened walls and collapsed roofs. The whole place smelled of ash and smoke. He coughed. "I don't know where to start. Any ideas?"

Dr. Mills was looking up a road that seemed to point toward Mt. Elgon's peak before curving to the east a few hundred meters up. She pointed. "I think that's the hospital. You can still see most of the word painted on the front wall."

Mitch looked. Indeed she was right. Several of the letters were obscured by black burns and smoke stains. "Are you thinking that if there was an outbreak here, we'd see some evidence of it in the hospital?"

"Exactly," Dr. Mills confirmed.

Mitch had four of his men head up to the hospital to make sure it was secure. "Let's give them a moment." He turned to address Dr. Mills. "Once they get up there, we'll drive the trucks over."

She nodded. "After yesterday, that sounds fine to me."

While they waited, Dr. Mills added, "If you can look past the destruction and forget about how many dead there must be—"

Mitch looked at Dr. Mills, "What?"

She was shaking her head. "I was going to say, it's beautiful here, but it was a stupid thought. It *was* beautiful here. Look at the houses, the huts, the buildings. Somebody systematically burned this whole town."

Mitch looked back at the charred structures. He looked up the street to see his hired gunmen checking inside houses and behind walls as they went. They were careful with their lives.

"I can't imagine how many died." Dr. Mills apparently couldn't stop thinking about the death toll. "How many people lived here, do you know?"

"A thousand, maybe, but most of them probably ran off in the fields and the forests before the fire. People aren't as helpless as they seem sometimes, and uneducated doesn't mean stupid. They can still see trouble and know how to get away from it." Mitch squinted up the street. His men were at the hospital, and one was waving for them to come. "I don't think we'll find as many dead as the destruction suggests."

They got back into the trucks and slowly rolled up the dirt road toward the hospital.

The smell of ash took on a different character as they passed what looked like a school: three rectangular buildings arranged around a central courtyard, dirt worn by the running feet of playing children. Through the broken out windows, Mitch saw charred, misshapen chaos. Tables, shelves, books, ceiling supports, and a couple of soccer balls among other bits of rubble—or so it appeared.

At the hospital, Mitch got out first and conferred with his man in charge. Reality was ready to prove wrong his calculation that there wouldn't be that many dead. Even as the man told him what was inside, Mitch looked over the concrete front porch that stood level with his chest, and through the burned door. The hospital's roof had not collapsed, though it had burned through in several sections, allowing sunlight to pour in on the blackened horror inside.

Mitch understood the change in the smell as he saw the bodies, charred in a crust of black, contorted, with arms and legs sticking at angles as though the people had been frozen mid-task. Fingers were spread wide. Horror stretched petrified faces. And Dr. Mills was beside him, mouthing something about the barbarity. Her coworker, Simmons, fell to his knees, pulled his filter mask away from his face and retched on the pavement.

Staring in through the doorway, view blocked only by metal hinges bolted to small pieces of a burnt wooden door,

Mitch couldn't begin to guess how many bodies lay inside. The whole village? Was that possible? He thought about the three school buildings and looked at them over his shoulder as he lifted a foot to the next of the steps. Were those shapes he'd seen through the windows of the school burnt bodies as well?

Dr. Mills passed him on the way up the steps and waded into the ash-layered ward, careful not to disturb the dead. Mitch came in behind, noticing the ashes weren't hot. Nothing smoldered.

"My God," Dr. Mills muttered.

Mitch just shook his head.

"Could they have been *that* afraid of the disease?" she questioned.

After a moment of quiet thought, Mitch replied, "You think these people were dead before they were burned?"

Shaking her head, Dr. Mills countered, "I think these people were burned alive."

Mitch looked at the countless dead. "How do you know?"

"Look at them." She pointed. "These people died in agony, trying to run, trying to escape. Dead people — that is, people who died prior to being burned — would not have been burned in these positions."

Mitch understood. "What about Ebola?"

Dr. Mills walked further into the blackened ward, shaking her head. Mitch didn't know if that was an answer to his question or an expression of despair at the brutality of man against man. He couldn't bring himself to follow her through the room. He turned and went back out onto the front porch, then looked around at all the burned structures down the slopes.

He looked at one of his men and motioned to the houses along the road up to the hospital. "When you guys were checking, were there burned bodies in those?"

The man nodded. "Some."

Mitch shook his head, thinking of the scale of the massacre.

One of the mercenaries came running around the corner of the building, speaking rapidly in a tongue Mitch didn't understand. But he caught one familiar word: *mzungu*.

The man standing beside Mitch turned toward him, pointing through the hospital. "They have found two whites near the trees."

They ran.

Chapter 62

Mitch knelt beside the boy. He was in his late teens, maybe early twenties, and in really bad shape. The girl lying a few feet away was clearly dead, though not burned. Her eyes were open. Blood had crusted around her mouth and nose. Her cotton blouse and pants were stained. Her mouth hung open, buzzing with flies and crawling with small insects. There was no hint of motion—she was gone—but the boy was at least breathing.

Mitch touched a hand to his mask, making sure it still covered his mouth and nose. "Go get the doctor," he told the man who'd come back with him. He put a gloved hand to the boy's shoulder and shook.

The boys red eyes snapped open and he coughed.

Mitch told another of the men to get some water for the boy. He then turned his attention back to the young man. "Can you hear me?"

The boy nodded, barely.

Mitch asked, "Are you Austin Cooper, from Denver?"

Austin tried to smile. His teeth were caked with blood and the remains from the last time he'd thrown up.

"Can you talk?"

Just then, the man arrived with a plastic bottle, half full of water.

Austin croaked unintelligibly. Mitch took the bottle and poured some into the boy's mouth. Austin closed his eyes and red-tinted tears flowed. He tried to speak again, but the words wouldn't come. Mitch poured a little more water into his mouth.

Dr. Mills came running up and dropped down at Austin's other side. "Oh, my God," she said. To one of the men, she instructed, "Go get Dr. Simmons." She put a gloved hand on Austin's face, and turned to Mitch. "He's got a fever."

"Ebola?" There was fear in Mitch's voice.

She looked down at Austin. She looked at the girl. She looked a back up at Mitch and nodded.

"Can you tell me what happened here?" Mitch asked Austin.

"Yes," Austin answered in a raspy voice.

The End

Book 2 in the Ebola K Trilogy will be out in late autumn of 2014.

If you'd like to join my email list the link is below. Or if you're into Liking, Pinning, or Following, the links to social media sites where you can do that are below. I try keep everyone up to date with upcoming releases… oh, who am I kidding. Mostly I post random silly crap that I find interesting or amusing.

My website

http://bobbyadair.com
http://bobbyadair.com/subscribe/

Facebook

https://www.facebook.com/BobbyAdairAuthor

Pinterest

http://www.pinterest.com/bobbyadairbooks/

Twitter

http://www.twitter.com/BobbyAdairBooks

On that whole question of reviews...

Every time a reader leaves a review, an aspiring author gets a new pencil.

Yeah, I know that line sucks but I've been in front of my computer proofreading for something like fourteen hours straight trying to get this book published before midnight and I'm half brain-fried. Eh, maybe I'll edit it out later with a better line. But, the whole point of this part is to beg for a moment of your time for a review.

I know, the word review is kind of intimidating but don't be intimidated. Any little bit of blabber qualifies. In fact, you can copy and paste this line, "This was the best book in the whole wide world!! It goes really well with the **Ebola Virus Plush Toy** here on Amazon!!"

Reviews help out indie authors more than you know.

Oh yeah, I almost forgot. *PLEASE*, leave a review on the website where you bought the book. My landlord likes it when I pay my rent on time. Reviews (especially the good ones) help make that happen.

This link might work for finding a place to leave a review.

Thanks for reading! – Bobby

Other Books by Bobby Adair

Horror

Slow Burn: Zero Day, book 1

Slow Burn: Infected, book 2

Slow Burn: Destroyer, book 3

Slow Burn: Dead Fire, book 4

Slow Burn: Torrent, book 5

Slow Burn Box Set: Destroyer and Dead Fire

And coming soon…a joint collaboration with T.W. Piperbrook

Satire

Flying Soup

64656966R00164